Cyclone

Tropic Storm, Volume 2

Kira Parke

Published by Kira Parke, 2018.

This is a work of fiction. Similarities to real people, places, or events are entirely coincidental.

CYCLONE

First edition. December 5, 2018.

Copyright © 2018 Kira Parke.

ISBN: 979-8230310754

Written by Kira Parke.

For anyone who has ever beaten the odds.

Chapter One:

Framework

Lydia approached the building site carrying a cooler she'd retrieved from the truck. She stopped to admire Dean, measuring, hammering and glistening in the sun. She loved it when he glistened. His tan was dark and his hair was bleached blonde, with all the time he was spending outdoors. The long scar on Dean's left cheek suited him; it made him look distinguished and more than a bit badass. Dean had always looked like a guy who could take care of business, but he'd buffed up even more over the last few months. He had been working out each morning like clockwork, doing chin-ups off of rafters and push-ups on the concrete slab. His arms and shoulders were larger than ever and Lydia couldn't help but stop and squeeze a muscle almost every time she passed the man. More importantly, Dean had strength of character and Lydia knew that he'd always look out for her. Their relationship hadn't started with a chance meeting at a party, or on a dating site. There had been running and danger and loss of life. He was her protector and she was his.

The frame of their new house was nearly complete, thanks to some hired hands, but mostly owing to the tireless efforts of Dean's mate: Ben Kelly. Dean and Ben had worked long days and many nights on the house, a fact that Lydia admired, but she was starting to feel the pinch. She and Dean hadn't spent much time together, away from the site, not for the last six months at least. Finding the right property had taken a couple of months in itself, then there was the administrative side of things and all sorts of unexpected preparation. Dean had experienced difficulties retaining laborers and of course there was the famous Far North Queensland weather. Storms and strong winds had destroyed the initial build, not once, but twice. Ben had come to the rescue on the third rebuild, after the remaining contractors had walked off the job. Progress came slowly, with Dean caught up in the sourcing of materials, as well as carpentry, plumbing and a little leftover electrical work. He'd funded the land purchase and everything else with the sale of his waterfront home, back in Surfer's Paradise; he was selfless like that. Lydia loved Dean all the more for his dedication to their new home, but she could see it was all taking a toll on him.

Waning sunlight filtered through a light blanket of cloud and the buzz of crickets had just begun. Fields of sugarcane burned in the distance, an infernal blanket of scorching red. Lydia's white, linen top clung to her chest and her neck felt almost feverish, even with her chestnut hair pulled up high. She wondered for a moment, if her denim shorts were too short. They weren't as revealing as the ones she saw the local girls wearing, but she could have sworn that Ben gave her a sly sideways glance as she approached. Lydia shyly looked away and pretended to survey the block. It was a square acre; large for what was still considered a suburb, even though to Lydia, Innisfail was more of a country town.

Amongst the lengthening shadows cast by palm trees, Lydia spotted a large, furry shape bounding through the long grass toward her. The open mouth, lolling tongue and wide eyes belonged to a hulking, beast of a dog that Dean had named: Captain. The animal skidded to a halt comically and jumped up on Lydia, licking her face eagerly. She scratched Captain's neck and chest and kissed him on the head. The colossal dog, launched himself off of Lydia's small frame and disappeared just as quickly as he had arrived. Lydia laughed and shook her head, continuing on toward Dean and Ben.

"Thought you blokes could use a beer," Lydia called out, whipping the lid off of the cooler for dramatic effect.

"Blokes? You're more Aussie than me now, Lyds," replied Ben, tucking his tape measure back into his tool belt.

Lydia threw a bottle at Ben, which he caught adroitly.

"You read my mind, lady," said Dean, wiping his brow with the back of his gloved hand.

Lydia kissed Dean and twisted the top off of an icy bottle. She took a swig and then handed the beer to him. "Yes, I did. There's some wicked stuff going on in there."

"You guys gonna' get X-rated? Maybe I'll head off," joked Ben.

He took a swig of his beer, most of it disappearing into his thick, brown beard. He leaned forward and let the liquid drip onto the ground.

"No, no. Not yet anyway. It's almost 'tools down' time for you guys, yeah?" suggested Lydia.

"Guess so," Dean responded, casting his eyes back over the site.

"Hey. You've done enough for today, okay?" Lydia said, turning his head back toward her with a finger on his stubbled chin.

"You're the foreman," replied Dean, smiling warmly. "We'll get that bracing sorted out first thing," Dean proclaimed to Ben. "Cyclone Season will be here before we know it."

"Guess I'll finish up at the pub," Ben interjected, chugging on his beer.

"Nonsense. Come back to the house with us. There's a roast chicken with your name on it," Lydia shot back.

"No offense, but who's cooking?" Ben queried, tugging at his beard thoughtfully.

"No need to panic, mate. My sister, Brianna's cooking tonight," Dean explained with a chuckle.

"Oh, good. Just curious is all, mate," Ben responded, looking relieved.

A woman with dark hair and skin appeared between a bougainvillea and a frangipani tree. She wore a colorful sarong and carried a large basket full of fruit. The woman, still cradling her cargo, picked a frangipani flower and placed it behind her right ear.

"Lani!" Lydia called out, waving eagerly.

"Hello everyone," Lani replied.

"Dean, you've met Lolani before and Lani, this is Ben," Lydia announced ceremoniously.

"Hi," Ben offered awkwardly.

"I had a lot of extra fruit off my trees that I thought you might like. I know you're hooked on mangoes, Lydia," Lolani explained warmly.

"That's so sweet of you," Lydia responded, hugging the woman.

"I didn't hear a car. Did you walk all the way here, Lani?" Dean questioned.

"Yes. It's not so far and It's a beautiful evening," she answered.

"See, Dean? Walking. It's a thing!" Lydia teased.

"Lydia and I work together," Lolani explained for Ben's benefit.

"Cool," Ben replied with his hands on his hips, as he kicked the dirt.

"The house looks great," Lolani complimented.

"Thanks very much. It's been a long road, but I think we're finally getting somewhere," replied Dean.

"You are very talented. All of you," Lolani said, looking at Dean, Lydia and Ben in turn.

"You're the real talent. You should see Lani's paintings, Dean. They're incredible," Lydia remarked, squeezing Lolani's arm affectionately.

She winced and pulled away. Lydia, perplexed, surveyed the woman's arm to find bruising that looked fresh.

"You okay?" Lydia enquired.

"Oh, yes Lydia. I fell when I was pruning my garden this morning. It's nothing," Lolani said smiling.

"Would you like to come to my sister's place for dinner?" Dean offered.

"Thank you, but no. I have to get back to Bertie. He'll starve without me," Lolani replied with a chuckle.

Lydia's expression darkened.

THE TRIO PULLED UP at Brianna's house with Captain pacing up and down expectantly in the back of the truck. As soon as the handbrake was engaged, the dog sprang out of the tray and onto the grass, barking at the group to follow.

"Someone can smell tucker," remarked Ben, spilling out of the backseat and dusting off his flannel shirt and work-shorts.

"Go on, mate. Go say hi to your aunty Bri," Dean said, pointing to the front door of the stilted house.

Captain hurled himself over the wooden fence and flew up the stairs, through the verandah, barking and scratching at the door.

"Reminds me of someone," quipped Lydia, sidling up to Dean and threading her arm through his.

"Only when you make that veal thing. It... ahhh... makes me a little hard," Dean whispered.

Ben grimaced, "Hey, hey! Innocent party present. If I throw up in there, it'll insult your sister!" he asserted.

"Mate, you haven't tried her veal," Dean volleyed back.

"You know how wrong that sounds, right?" Lydia replied.

"I'm... I'm sticking with it," Dean affirmed, his straight face faltering until he finally cracked up.

The curtains parted at the window closest to the front door and a small face draped with strawberry blonde hair appeared. The face vanished, the door flew open and Captain disappeared inside, barking excitedly. Out of the doorway spilled a slight figure that ran down the stairs, across the yard finally colliding with Dean and Lydia.

"Uncle Dean! Aunty Lydia!"

"Tiny, little Faye, smallest of all beings," announced Dean, picking up the child and spinning her around.

"How are you, baby?" enquired Lydia.

"Good. I helped Mum make chicken and then I made potato salad and it sucked so I made coleslaw instead," rattled Faye without taking a breath.

"Are you supposed to say words like that?" queried Dean.

"Like what?" asked Faye.

"Chicken," answered Dean, winking at Lydia.

"Uncle Dean!" exclaimed Faye.

"I don't know. We always said 'chook' when I was growing up," Dean responded, flipping Faye around so that he was holding her by the ankles.

Faye planted her hands on the grass and steadied herself, "Uncle Dean, I'm gonna' do the starfish. Now let go!" she yelled.

Dean released his grip and Faye walked on her hands for a moment before deftly flipping herself upright.

"Uh, how is that a starfish?" whispered Ben.

"Ours is not to question the starfish, but to embrace it," Lydia responded.

"Well said," Dean added.

Lydia and Dean clapped and Ben placed his pinky fingers in his mouth and whistled loudly. Faye scrutinized the tall bearded man and ran back into the house.

"Did I whistle outta' tune?" Ben asked incredulously.

"Nah, mate. She just thinks you're ugly," quipped Dean.

Ben began dancing around like a boxer, throwing punches at Dean without connecting. Dean wrapped a muscled arm around Ben's neck and pretend-punched him in the face repeatedly.

"Guys, guys! Is this for my benefit? I'm swooning, so you can stop now," pleaded Lydia jokingly.

The two men separated, Ben holding his hands up in mock surrender.

"Alright, mate. You win this one. In my defense, though, I still get plenty of action. Picked up just the other night, in fact. A little lady named: Danica," oozed Ben.

"Uh huh. Sounds made up to me. Do we get to meet this... what was her name?" Dean asked.

"Danica."

"Danica. Right."

"Yep. You can meet her tonight if you want. I might get her to pick me up later, seeing as how my bike's-"

"In the shop," Dean and Lydia repeated in unison.

"If it wasn't for that shop, me and your boyf' here would never have met. You can't say that I haven't had a positive impact on your lives now, can you?" Ben teased.

"Yeah, well Dean should have maybe been more... selective in his choice of bike repair providers?" Lydia said, not completely in jest.

"They're the best on the coast," Dean responded with childlike sincerity.

"Anyway, with that bike of yours always in pieces, maybe you can learn to enjoy walking, like me," Lydia japed.

"Yeah, why is your ride always busted?" Dean questioned.

"She's complicated," Ben said smiling.

"Are we talking about Danica now, or the bike?" Lydia questioned.

"My bike," Ben clarified, sounding a little put out.

The trio walked up the stairs, through the verandah and entered Brianna's house. Faye was performing the starfish down the hallway and Dean's twin sister was busily setting the table. Lydia placed the basket of tropical fruit onto a side-table in the dining room. The air was scented with freshly cut gardenias and good food. The place was furnished with mismatched pieces that had been lovingly reconditioned by Dean since his arrival. There were framed pictures of

Brianna, Faye and Dean all over the place, but none of their parents. After what Dean had revealed about his childhood back when they'd first met, Lydia wasn't surprised that there were no remembrances of their upbringing in the house. It felt to Lydia as though Brianna and Dean had forged a family unit of their own, one where parents weren't entirely necessary, from a very young age. They'd spent years apart as adults, but then again, they'd shared the kind of intuition that only twins can really know.

She was an inch shy of Dean's height, but Brianna had the same slightly olive hued skin and brown hair flecked with sun-bleached blonde. Her eyes were lighter, more of an amber color than brown and her lips had a similar shapeliness about them. Her frame was solid and her breasts were naturally huge. Lydia was slightly jealous of Brianna's attributes, only ever filling a B-cup herself. Ben had trouble not gawking at Brianna's bust, that was until Dean scowled at him, hard enough to make him pretend to look for Captain in the kitchen. The dog was in the corner, near the stove, gnawing on a large bone, unaware of anyone or anything else.

"You finally made it up the stairs!" called Brianna, finally looking up from her place settings.

"Long day. How you going, Bri?" Dean explained as he ambled over to his sister and gave her a long hug.

"I'm great, D. I gave Cap a beef bone I got from the butcher. Don't want him anywhere near chicken bones, not after last time," said Brianna, looking in Lydia's direction. "How's the new castle coming along?" she asked, her chin on Dean's broad shoulder.

"All good. Especially with Ben working, well, semi-hard," Dean japed.

"First of all, I'm the best, and only, laborer you got. Also, please never say 'hard' or even 'semi-hard' in my presence," Ben returned as he pushed Dean away from Brianna and kissed her on the cheek.

"This one's allowed to kiss me all he wants," Brianna purred, slapping Ben on the butt.

"Do you need any help?" Lydia offered.

"Nope," Brianna responded curtly.

Lydia looked at Dean and Ben looked away awkwardly. Brianna wiped her hands on a dish cloth and strolled back into the kitchen. Faye cartwheeled her way back to the dining area and wrapped her skinny arms around Lydia's legs.

"*I* like you," whispered Faye, looking straight up into Lydia's face.

"And I like *you* too," Lydia responded affectionately.

Faye looked sideways at Ben and he smiled goofily at her, crossing his eyes and flapping grimy hands on either side of his face like fish fins. Faye bolted to the bathroom and slammed the door.

"Really?" Dean queried.

"I'm digging deep into my kid-friendly material now, mate. She's a tough audience," Ben shot back.

"She's six-years old, Benjamin. Don't take it too personally," added Lydia.

"D!" called Brianna from the kitchen. Dean shot Lydia a glance and proceeded toward his sister.

"You beckoned?" stated Dean as he converged on Brianna, who was busy carving up two large, roasted chickens.

"You wanna' give me some warning before you bring guests over?" Brianna whispered.

"What happened to 'this one's welcome anytime' and all of that?" Dean whispered back.

"Faye's terrified of him. I think she thinks he's like... you know, that Mason guy you described so bloody vividly. It's like you enjoy scaring your niece. Anyway, I was just being polite," Brianna replied. "Just like I am with your little girlfriend out there."

"We don't mention *his* name. Also, *her* name's Lydia," Dean lobbed back.

"She's trouble. She'll bring her problems up here, you watch. I'm terrified all the time. I keep telling my daughter to look out for that man, because I'm scared that he'll show up one day and take her or something. I love you D, but my first priority will always be Faye, you know that."

"Look, Bri, you've been great, helping us like you have. I said we could stay at a motel or the pub if this got too much for you," Dean said.

Brianna spun around to face Dean, gripping a chicken leg like a weapon. "I'm not having my brother stay at a motel!" she said softly but harshly.

"What's the real problem here?"

Brianna threw the chicken leg back into the large, roasting tray. "I'm just looking out for us: you, me and Faye. We're blood and nothing trumps that. Not damaged little girls, not anything. You've got a good heart, especially considering where we came from. I don't want to see anyone taking advantage of you."

"Look at me. Do you think anyone's taking advantage of this?" Dean quipped, casting a muscle pose and furrowing his brow.

"I know you're this... tough guy, or whatever. I hope she's not your Achilles-heel."

"Hey. Everything's fine. You worry too much. You're a mum, I get it. You're just not *my* mum, okay? I love you, even though you drive me frickin' insane," Dean said tenderly, as he rubbed Brianna's shoulder.

"Maybe tell your buddy to shave or something," Brianna added, grinning.

AFTER DINNER, BRIANNA began scraping, stacking and clearing plates, with Faye's help. Lydia didn't wait for an okay before hopping up to ferry glasses and serving platters to the kitchen. Brianna kept her head down, not making eye contact with Lydia as they worked. Dean stood up to offer some assistance but was waved down by Lydia just as fast as he had arisen. A knock at the door sent Captain hurtling up the hallway with a clickety-clack of claws to floor. Ben bounded over and unlocked the front entrance. The big dog made a noise that sounded something like disapproval at not being pre-warned about more visitors.

"Come on in, love," said Ben to the newcomer.

"I come earlier, but text you send is for wrong address."

"Well, you're here now. Danny, this is my mate: Dean. Dean this is the lovely Danica," offered Ben.

"Very please to meet you, Den," purred Danica, looking Dean up and down.

"Same," said Dean, rising to shake Danica's hand gently.

"Hi!" exclaimed Lydia, barreling out of the kitchen, skidding to a halt and coming face to face with the tall, shapely woman.

Ben threw an arm around Danica's slender shoulders as she caressed her bare stomach, left exposed by a very tight mid-riff top. Danica's firm hips and behind were on full display in almost transparent, purple leggings. Her neck-length hair was dyed bright red and tousled to look like she'd just come from a quick romp in the hay. She parted her heavily glossed lips and looked at Dean, then back at Lydia, before smiling smugly.

"And you are?" Danica enquired coldly.

"Dean's partner. I'm Lydia Hawkins. We live here but we're building a house nearby. We're all one happy family I guess you could say," prattled Lydia, instantly wishing that her ears weren't glowing red.

"Is funny how you Oossies call boyfriend and girlfriend... how you say?"

"Partner, you mean?" offered Ben.

"Yes. Is like you are in business and not in bed together in literal vay," replied Danica, smoothing out her top by brushing her manicured hands over her firm, high breasts.

Lydia surveyed the perfect landscape of Danica's impossible body. The woman looked like a cartoon. Lydia huffed internally when she noted that Danica wasn't wearing a bra; she didn't need one. Sensing the growing awkwardness, Ben placed a guiding hand on the small of Danica's toned lower back and moved her to the kitchen where he introduced her to Brianna. Lydia cringed at hearing the cordial tone in Brianna's voice; the polar opposite to the frigid reception reserved for herself. Danica said a few patronizing words to Faye, apparently not good with talking to children. Lydia's animosity doubled.

Ben leant backwards and called out to Dean, "You still wanna' head to the site for that thing," he said.

"Uh, yeah," Dean responded, standing up and brushing imaginary debris from his jeans. Danica beamed like a child who'd just been told school was cancelled for all eternity.

"What's this?" enquired Lydia.

"Oh, nothing to worry about, lady. Just gotta' check something. If I don't, I'll worry about it all night," Dean said with an easy smile.

"Okay. You don't need any help?" Lydia returned, a hint of pleading in her voice.

"No, no. You stay here and relax. If I need you, I'll give you a buzz."

"Okay," replied Lydia, a little defeated. She didn't relish the thought of being in the house without Dean; he was the buffer between her and Brianna.

Dean, Ben and Danica said their goodbyes, pealing out of the front door and into the night. Lydia watched Brianna amble back into the kitchen, her fraying, old house-dress a testament to how hard-done-by she claimed to be, since the arrival of her unexpected live-in guests. More precisely, the problem she'd had was with Lydia; Dean was always welcome. In fairness, Dean did just show up unannounced with Lydia in tow, some eight months prior. They had little choice after everything that had happened back in Surfer's. An image of Dora's bloody corpse penetrated Lydia's thoughts. She felt the oppressive weight of costing her best friend her life. Dora would never have accused Lydia of such a thing, but it felt like gravel under Lydia's skin. Maybe Brianna was right to treat her like the burden she undoubtedly was.

Lydia retreated to the guest room that she and Dean shared, at the rear of the house, and threw herself on the bed. She pulled her sketchpad and charcoals from the bedside table and began to draw. She drew a woman's form, with long, slender legs, round hips and teased hair. The woman had a look of abject horror on her face, the source of which was revealed as Lydia sketched: a giant crocodile with jagged teeth and its jaws agape, charged at the woman with a predatory look in its reptilian eye.

"Oh, vhat horror! I'm going to be, how do you say? Eaten! Eeeeeek!" Lydia performed to herself, cackling.

"Whatcha' doing, Aunty Lydia?" asked Faye, appearing at the bedroom door.

"Just... amusing myself," Lydia responded.

"Who's that? Crap-nuts! Is that Darneeka?" enquired Faye, her eyes widening as she studied the picture Lydia was adding finishing touches to.

"Language! And... yes. Do you like it?" asked Lydia, holding up the drawing to show Faye properly.

"It's awesome! Needs blood though. And her boobies are bigger."

"They're not that big," Lydia shot back, smiling and pulling Faye in for a hug.

"I don't like her and I'm not that keen on Ben neither," Faye mumbled, pushing her face into Lydia's armpit.

"Not that keen? I swear you are six going on thirty-six, child. What don't you like about Dar-nee-ka?" Lydia asked, affecting a vaguely European accent.

"She talks like Dracklia. And she makes all the men look at her. But Uncle Dean's not like that and you're prettier than her. I wish I was pretty like you when I grow up."

Lydia tucked a stray strawberry blonde lock behind Faye's ear. "Okay, baby, it's actually: Dracula, and thank you for the compliment. You are very pretty already and you don't need to look like anyone but you okay?"

"Darc-u-la. Okay. Are you going to live with us forever, Aunty Lydia?"

Lydia chuckled. "You know we're building a house of our own, your Uncle Dean and I. But we'll be close by and we want you to come over whenever you want, okay?"

Faye stared into Lydia's eyes and stood up on the bed. She pulled Lydia's cheeks back and forth, making a wet flapping sound erupt from her mouth. Faye giggled hysterically and bounced up and down on the mattress.

"Okay, I guess. Will you draw me?"

"You got it," Lydia replied.

Lydia sat Faye on the bed before taking a seat on the floor with her sketchpad. She flipped to a fresh page and started roughing out an outline. Faye gave her a gap-toothed smile, her ruddy cheeks like plums.

"What's going on here? Faye, it's bedtime, go and brush your teeth," ordered Brianna, leaning against the doorframe.

"Just a couple minutes Mum! I'm getting my porcher done!" Faye argued.

"Portrait! And no, forget it. You've got school tomorrow and I'm not dealing with a cranky little lady tomorrow morning, I'm just not!" Brianna countered.

"Mum!" protested Faye.

"Get!" fired Brianna, pointing a stern finger down the corridor, toward the bathroom.

"Night, Aunty Lydia," said Faye, forlornly dragging her feet out of the guest room door past her mother.

"She's not your aunty. Dean and her aren't married," Brianna huffed as she wandered off after her daughter.

Lydia threw her sketchpad onto the bed and stood up to close the door. Just then, a high-pitched ring filled the room and Lydia pulled her phone from her pocket to see Dean's name on the screen.

"You'd better come to the building site. Something's happened!" Dean announced, sounding out of breath.

Chapter Two:

Echoes

Lydia jumped in the truck and sped off to the site, not knowing what to expect. She tried her best to suppress the fear that her past had come back to haunt her, yet again. In her mind, Mason's intense, bearded face loomed large, as though he were watching her every move. Neither her nor Dean had any real weapons, though the building site was full of them, wasn't it? Hopefully it wasn't too late. A bark from the back of the vehicle took Lydia by surprise. She looked in the rear-view and was greeted by Captain's happy-looking face.

"How did you get back there? I didn't even see you jump in!" Lydia yelled, delighted for the back-up. "We're definitely going to need you tonight, Cap."

Lydia pulled up to the property and surreptitiously climbed out of the truck, whistling for Captain to accompany her. The dog's ears shot straight up and he bolted for the building site, making low, rumbly noises with every foot-fall. Lydia felt a prickly sensation traveling up her neck and she slowly followed Captain's path to whatever awaited her. She could see the faint glow of lights in and around the house frame. It looked like Dean had maybe lit the place to better see whatever it was that he came to check up on, but he hadn't used the usual halogen lamps; perhaps they had been vandalized. The place was eerily silent, not even Captain could be heard and Lydia felt very alone all of a sudden. A shriek overhead made Lydia jump, as a flock of Flying Foxes flapped their leathery wings and chattered excitedly as they searched for food. The moon cast a sickly light over the landscape and the odd rustle in the tall grass made Lydia internally beg for Dean to find her quickly.

Lydia cautiously walked through the empty, front doorframe and into the tarpaulin covered space. There was a feeling that some sort of scuffle had occurred as tools were strewn about and the area was in general disarray. Lydia padded almost silently from room to room, barely even breathing. Suddenly, a heavy 'thump' stopped her in her tracks and Lydia looked down to see an enormous bullfrog staring back up at her. She clutched her chest and walked around the creature, relieved that the disturbance was nothing insidious. It was already too late, when Lydia detected the presence of another. From out of nowhere, arms wrapped around her torso. She struggled, but the stranger's grip only tightened. Lydia managed to drop, using her body-weight to escape her assailant's grasp. She rounded on the shadowy figure and brought a knee up to its crotch. The figure brought a muscled arm down fast, blocking Lydia's attack.

"Whoa, whoa! You don't want to damage that, do you?" exclaimed the stranger.

"You stinker!" Lydia shot back, slapping an open hand against the man's chest.

"Who were you expecting?"

"Let's not go into it. You scared the hell out of me!" Lydia cried.

"I know. I'm sorry. Had to be done."

"Had to be done? Captain! Kill!" Lydia called. Captain trotted over from out of the shadows and looked up at Dean, before jumping up on him and panting into his face.

"Okay, dog breath. Go and look for cane toads, mate," Dean said chuckling and pushing the large dog away. "Me and your mum have important stuff to do.

The dog padded off obediently into the night and Dean placed an arm across Lydia's shoulders.

"Come on, lady. Let's go this way," Dean instructed.

Dean walked Lydia into what was to later become the living room. The space was subtly lit with long, beeswax candles and an ornately carved, wooden table was set in the middle. A bottle of champagne, in an ice bucket, sat on a purpose-built stand and dessert had been served at each of the place settings. A vase overflowing with irises adorned the middle of the table and there were two beautifully crafted chairs to complete the scene.

Lydia wiped tears from her eyes and turned to embrace Dean. She placed both hands behind his head and pulled him close before kissing him deeply.

"I'm speechless," said Lydia huskily.

"You don't need to say anything, just sit," Dean stated.

Dean pulled a chair out for Lydia and popped open the champagne. He poured a glass for Lydia and then himself.

Raising his glass, Dean toasted, "To my favorite woman in the world, may she care for and not assault my crotch, lest the Connors name die with me!"

Lydia giggled, "That's the toast you're going with?"

"Sure am. Okay, look, I'm not going to stand here and blow smoke up your... uh... shorts," began Dean.

"Poetry," joked Lydia.

"But I love you like I've never loved anyone else. And I don't want to live without you in my life, so-" Dean stopped abruptly and whistled loudly. "Captain!" he called.

The dog lumbered into the room carrying a small, velvet pouch in his mouth which he deposited into Dean's eager hand.

"Good boy," Dean said, stroking Captain's broad head.

Pulling open the drawstrings, Dean pulled out a small, beautifully fashioned, wooden box. He snapped it open to reveal a wooden ring, the color of honey. The ring had been set with an intricate flower, an iris, carved of rosewood and lacquered to a brilliant gloss.

Leaving his seat, dropping to one knee and proffering the ring to Lydia, Dean asked, "Would you-"

"Oh God, yes!" interjected Lydia, jumping up and throwing her arms around Dean, kissing him repeatedly.

Captain barked and ran around in circles as Dean scooped Lydia up in his arms. He carefully deposited her back onto her chair before taking a seat himself.

"Creme Brulee?" Lydia enquired.

"Don't worry. Bri made it," Dean explained.

Lydia picked up a spoon and tapped at the hard sugar coating, cracking it. She stared at the custard erupting like lava through the shards.

"So, it's not laced with arsenic?" Lydia joked, peering at Dean through her lashes.

"No. Least, I don't think so. If Bri was gonna' knock you off, I think she'd use cyanide. It's more theatrical," Dean countered.

"All critics aside, Dean Connors, I love you."

"I'm... growing fond of you too," replied Dean.

Lydia twisted in her seat, open mouthed, and flicked a spoonful of Brulee at Dean's face.

"That's it!" Dean shouted, as he lunged at Lydia.

Lydia squealed and propelled herself out of her chair in one fluid movement. Dean made after her and Lydia ran out of the living area and into the night. She rounded the house frame, running into the rear of the property. Lydia could hear the crunching of grass approaching from the other side of the house, so she ran in the opposite direction. Looking behind her, she saw that the source of the sound was Captain. Lydia's shoulders drooped and she breathed a sigh of relief. All of a sudden, she let out a stilted scream as Dean intercepted her, materializing from the darkness silently.

"You're still wearing dessert," Lydia quipped as Dean pulled her close.

"I saved it for you," Dean responded.

Lydia leaned in and extended her tongue before hooking her foot behind Dean's knee and pulling back to force him to the ground. She whistled and Captain rushed over, eagerly sniffing Dean's face, before licking the custard off of his forehead.

"Okay," Dean said, wincing. "You win this one, lady."

"Damn right I do," remarked Lydia, stifling a giggle.

Lydia proffered a helping hand and Dean grabbed it. He started to rise to his feet before pulling Lydia down on top of him. The pair lay there on the cool grass without saying a word. Lydia could feel Dean's steady, powerful heartbeat against her chest and she closed her eyes. She rested her head on his shoulder and in that moment, everything was as she felt it should be. There were no vengeful ex-partners, no resentful sisters and no European vixens. She and Dean were the only two people in the world. The buzzing of cicadas faded into a soothing rhythm and a fresh breeze cut through the humidity.

Lydia unbuttoned Dean's navy, linen shirt and traced the phoenix tattoo emblazoned over both pectorals with a fingertip before kissing her way down past his sternum to his hard stomach. She tugged at his thick belt buckle and pulled his button-fly open nimbly, reaching into his boxers with eager fingers and stroking his hardness until his pelvis began to move. Lydia glanced up at Dean's face seductively before moving her mouth lower and lower, teasing him until she could feel his desire reaching its peak. Lydia took him into her mouth as she ran her hands up over Dean's abdomen. She massaged his hardness with her tongue, as her lips enveloped him. Dean's breathing quickened and he couldn't take his eyes off of Lydia, barely even hazarding a blink.

When she had taken him to the edge, Lydia stood up and slowly shimmied out of her shorts. She took off her top and ran her fingertips over her erect nipples, moaning gently. She smiled coyly, enjoying the appreciative audience. Lydia lowered herself down onto Dean and he pulled her forward, his warm mouth on her breasts. Then, in one swift movement, Dean flipped Lydia onto her back. He moved downward, positioning himself between her legs, kissing the delicate skin on the inside of her thighs. He smoothly pulled her underwear down and off. Lydia's back arched as Dean's tongue explored her, flicking at her most intimate places. He devoured her greedily, like he had never tasted anything quite as good. Lydia couldn't help but grasp at his head and pull his hair, as Dean brought her to shuddering completion. She lay there, basking in her own glow for a time, staring at the lover she desired more than anyone. Dean slid up and lay next to her, leaning over to look into her eyes.

Lydia climbed onto Dean's hard body, running her hands over his impressive physique, then she gingerly guided Dean into her. She began to move rhythmically as Dean's hands massaged her breasts. Dean sounded like a wild beast as he lifted his hips off the ground and met her gyrations with complimentary force. Joined together, time seemed to stretch and contract and Lydia wished the moment could last for eternity. A wave of sublime heat rushed from between her thighs, radiating up into her as she climaxed, harder than she ever had before.

LYDIA'S RECURRING NIGHTMARES of Mason had long departed and now she dreamed of her mother, her sister and more often: Dora. She would mostly see Dora hovering over her, red hair tendrils shimmering as though she were underwater. Her deep, soulful eyes sad and searching Lydia's face, always, searching for answers. Her skin was deathly pale and her clothing still torn where Mason's blade had entered her again and again. The strangest thing was: there was no blood. Dora would speak, most nights, but her voice sounded far off, like a radio that was turned down just a little too low. She would always talk in half-sentences, and Lydia felt as though she had missed something important. Her dreams were lucid and Lydia felt almost hyper-aware inside of them, like they were more than just subconscious images.

"... and maladies strike in threes," was what Dora kept saying over and over again.

Lydia tossed and turned and muttered things in her sleep. When she would get too restless, Dean would stroke her arm or hold her until she settled down. Sometimes Lydia would hear things moving through the house and she wasn't completely sure if they were in her head or not. She would lay there awake, her eyes closed, daring herself to open them for a look. Lydia imagined an entire bestiary of hags, ghouls and dead things wandering from room to room. She would often curse herself, wishing she had a less virile imagination; the inventions of her mind were ghastly. The nights seemed to go on for far too long and Lydia often longed for morning.

Lydia groaned as morning sunlight burned through her eyelids. She tugged at the covers as they slowly receded like the outgoing tide. She felt around for Dean, convinced that he was stealing the quilt, but he wasn't there. Lydia opened one eye and the image of Captain, dragging her bed clothes off of her with his teeth, slowly came into focus.

"Okay, okay. I'm getting up," Lydia croaked.

Captain barked to hurry her up before wheeling around and trotting out the bedroom door, presumably to the kitchen.

"Bad dog," Lydia scolded huskily.

Lydia made her way to the kitchen to find Brianna unpacking grocery items. Not feeling up to dealing with Dean's sister just yet, Lydia took a detour toward the front verandah. Dean stood there, silhouetted in the morning sunlight. He was wearing a dark grey tee shirt, with the sleeves cut off, and black jeans.

"You're a welcome sight, Dean Connors," Lydia cooed, throwing her arms around the man's neck.

"Get dressed. We're going out," Dean stated with a smile.

"No building today?" Lydia enquired with a hint of surprise.

"Today we're jigging," Dean answered.

"Okay. That's another Australian thing, I'm guessing, Dean-o-dile Dundee."

"Jigging's what we used to do when it was more of a surfing day than a school day," Dean explained.

"Okay. What should I wear?"

"As little as possible. Also, prepare to get wet."

"Sounds good to me."

THE BIKE POWERED DOWN the highway and Lydia held onto Dean's waist with all of her strength. She loved feeling the warmth of him against her; it made her feel as though she belonged. The sound of the bike's gears was a rhythm Lydia had come to love. The sounds and smells of the engine had become synonymous with the man himself. She felt a tingle in the pit of her stomach whenever she thought of Dean. Sometimes Lydia felt a little embarrassed of her schoolgirl reaction to the man; she was in her thirties after all. But there was something about him, something rugged and classical, as though he'd just stepped out of an old movie. Lydia squeezed her eyes shut and giggled.

Trees and houses whipped by as they sped past countless road signs. The sky was cloudless and enormous and the sun burnt relentlessly. They had been lucky with the weather of late; Innisfail had a reputation as one of the wettest places in the country. Lydia hazarded the thought that maybe things were turning around for her and her husband to be. It felt strange in the most wonderful way to envisage herself as a wife; Lydia had never been one before. She'd been virtually a hostage to the worst kind of man, but that was a relationship predicated on fear. It felt right to be in a partnership that was based on respect and love.

Lydia's thin dress flapped in the wind and she feared it would be ripped off her body at any moment. After a time, the bike turned left and a distinctive ocean scent permeated the air. Tall Norfolk Pines loomed over the road and teens wearing swimsuits with towels draped around their necks ambled toward the water.

"Jigging," Lydia whispered to herself as they pulled up near the beach.

Lydia dismounted and took off her helmet. Dean unzipped his leather riding jacket and smiled at her happily.

"Mission Beach, lady. This is what it's all about," Dean proclaimed as he dropped his jeans, revealing the boardshorts he'd been wearing underneath.

"Oh, that's adorable," Lydia remarked.

Dean stuffed his clothes into one of the pannier bags on his bike and secured his keys in a waterproof capsule that he wore around his neck via a leather cord.

"What's going on under that dress?" Dean queried, looking Lydia up and down.

Lydia turned her head, allowing the ocean breeze to blow her hair over her face, feigning shyness. She then threw off her dress to reveal a floral print bikini.

"Holy hell!" Dean exclaimed sincerely.

"You like that, huh?" Lydia quizzed, suddenly feeling a little self-conscious.

"Are you kidding? You're blindingly beautiful, Lydia."

"Oh, come on," Lydia teased.

"I'm serious. I'm blinder than a welder's dog over here."

"Don't change," Lydia responded, pressing her body against Dean's and kissing him deeply.

"Hey, lady. Look," Dean stated, pointing at the water.

Lydia squealed and bolted toward the ocean, Dean following behind. Just as Dean's feet made contact with the sand, something caught his attention. The obnoxious rumble of a chopper, slowing on its arrival to the parking area made Dean turn around cautiously. He studied the rider, but he couldn't make out any recognizable colors or symbols. The guy might have been a lone bike enthusiast, it was hard to tell. Dean felt his pulse race a little, but the stranger didn't look his way. Dean shook it off and continued to chase after Lydia. She was jumping around in the shallows when Dean caught up to her and picked her up, spinning her around effortlessly. Suddenly Lydia's expression changed to one of shock.

"No!" she cried, before Dean pulled back and then threw her into the water.

Lydia shot up and wiped sea water from her eyes and smoothed her hair out.

"That's it!" Lydia howled, sweeping Dean's legs out from under him with one kicking motion.

Dean fell backward into the water, laughing, and Lydia ran. Dean sprang up and gave chase, Lydia sprinting to stay ahead of him. They ran the length of the beach, their pace slowing as they gradually ran out of steam. Soon they came to Clump Point and they disappeared into the trees.

"This is beautiful!" Lydia exclaimed, slowing to a walking pace.

"Yeah, it's not bad," Dean responded.

"Oh, you are a man without passion," Lydia jibed.

"I don't know. My passion flares up now and again, depending on the situation at hand," Dean answered.

"What does that mean?" Lydia quizzed, turning to look at Dean.

Dean scooped Lydia up and then laid her down on a thicket of soft grass. He kissed her mouth, enjoying the softness of her lips and her hands on his back. He kissed Lydia's neck and her body tightened in response, a moan escaping her throat. Dean's mouth moved down across her collarbone and he pulled her bikini top down to reveal the soft skin of her breasts. He licked at a nipple, before taking it into his mouth, drawing on it and making Lydia's chest thrust toward him. Running his hands down her sides, Dean ran his tongue over her belly, stopping to lap at her navel. Lydia's breath quickened and she ran her fingers through Dean's hair, her hips beginning to gyrate.

Dean tugged at the ties on either side of Lydia's bikini bottoms and Lydia suddenly felt very aware that they were in a public place.

"No, no. People will see," Lydia protested half-heartedly.

"I don't care," Dean answered.

Dean kissed the inside of Lydia's thighs, licking and biting his way up and down until she was on the verge of begging. Sensing her near-desperation, Dean pulled Lydia's swimsuit away and teased at her with the hard tip of his tongue. He traced the outline of her until she pushed his head closer and then he went to work. Painting her with his tongue, entering her gradually with it, then circling the most sensitive part of her until Lydia was bucking upward and shuddering all over. He licked her with increasing pressure, changing the direction of stimulation when he sensed sensitivity was waning, Dean ate her like a tropical fruit. Lydia felt like she was rapidly approaching a cliff's edge, a cliff she desperately wanted to hurl herself off of. She continued to be propelled forward until finally, Lydia launched over the precipice. Her body exploded and she felt as though she were being showered with ecstatic sparks. It felt like she was falling for the longest time, until finally she lurched back into her own waiting body. She felt tender and renewed and a little drunk.

Dean smiled up at her with a contented look. He looked vaguely proud of himself as he helped Lydia redress herself.

"You're... you're something else, Deek Onners," Lydia mumbled with a goofy grin on her face.

"Happy?" Dean enquired, sidling up to Lydia.

"Oh, fuck yeah."

THE NEXT MORNING, AFTER showering and brushing her teeth, Lydia gathered some breakfast things and sat at the dining table alone.

She crunched her way through a bowl of muesli and sipped at coffee to a soundtrack of laughing Kookaburras. Early morning drizzle had dissipated and wind rattled the fly-screens on all the open windows. The sporadic sound of people bidding loved ones' goodbye for the day echoed down the street. She guessed that Brianna was out shopping or something and Faye would have been dropped off at school already. Lydia smiled to herself as she recounted the events of the previous two days. She held out her hand and looked at her ring; it was the most beautiful thing she had ever seen. Dean had promised to buy her a diamond as soon as he could, but Lydia begged him to let her keep the one he'd made with his own two hands. Dean. He was already at the building site undoubtedly, laboring over their future. How had her life transformed so perfectly and so quickly? Her thoughts then turned to Dora and she felt the crushing weight of guilt; it was a feeling she knew she would never shake, nor did she want to.

After washing up her breakfast dishes, Lydia walked into town as she always did on Thursdays and Fridays. She crossed the beautiful, cool looking water of the South Johnstone river and increased her pace when a black and white currawong dropped out of a gum tree and swooped her. Her shorts and tank top attracted a few stares from local males, as she quickly traversed the main street. She took her cap off and pulled her hair back and tied it off with an elastic she had 'borrowed' from Brianna's drawer in the bathroom vanity unit. It was a becoming a very muggy day and Lydia couldn't wait to get inside and enjoy some air conditioning. Her knapsack was already creating a sweat patch on her back and the soles of her feet burned in her sneakers. She reached around and pulled her water bottle from the side pocket of her bag. After pouring half of the contents onto her hatted head, she guzzled the remainder. It wasn't an unusual thing to do in the hotter parts of the country, Dean had told her. He often filled a wide brimmed cowboy-looking hat with water, before slamming it down onto his head.

Suddenly, the hairs on Lydia's neck stood up and she had the distinct feeling she was being watched. She scanned the street until she spotted the culprit across the road, pretending to look at postcards out the front of a mixed-business store. Lydia's instinct was to keep moving, but looking at her watch, she realized she had some time up her sleeve. She hated the idea of slinking away as though *she* had done something wrong. Lydia squeezed her hands into fists and walked across the road.

"Danica? Hi! So good to see you!" Lydia exclaimed.

"Oh, yes. Olivia. Is good to see you also," replied Danica, spinning the postcard display.

"Lydia. Doing some shopping?" Lydia enquired cordially.

"I send cardpost to family, in Ukraine," Danica said mechanically as she spun the display again, a little too hard. A middle-aged man pushing a baby in a pram twisted his head around like an owl as he passed the pair on the sidewalk. Danica arched her back, thrusting her perfect breasts outward and releasing what sounded like a moan of pleasure.

"Well that's a lovely thought. They must miss you. You're heading back sometime soon?" Lydia asked eagerly.

"No. I have visa extension. You must know all what I'm saying?" Danica added.

"Yeah, well, you and me both. You must be homesick, though, Danny. I mean, America is not unlike Australia in some ways, but the Ukraine... it must feel like you're on a different planet," Lydia said, instantly regretting it. She suddenly felt very bitchy.

"Danica. Only Ben call me Danny. Not place, but people are like, how you say? Alley-ans?"

"Aliens. I guess so. Hey, look, have a good day, Danica. Try and stay cool," said Lydia, amiably touching Danica's arm for effect.

Lydia felt as though maybe she had misjudged Danica. It was only natural that she felt protective over her relationship with Dean though, wasn't it? Danica certainly was a bit of a minx, but it was all too easy to paint her as the villain. Lydia looked back at Danica wiggling her way down the road in blue, almost transparent leggings. She felt a little sad for Danica in that moment; it was hard to be so far away from family. Lydia thought of Kitty and their mom. Would she see them anytime soon? She had felt safe enough giving Kitty the Innisfail address when she'd found out that Mason was remanded in custody. She thought Kitty might write her, in the old-fashioned pen to paper way, and maybe update her on Mom's condition. Part of her hoped that maybe her mom and sister might be able to live with her in Australia some day; they could make it work.

"You're a deep thinker, love. I can see that," said an older woman, sitting at a stall on the sidewalk.

"I don't know how deep I really am," responded Lydia, ambling over to the woman as though she was compelled to.

The woman had wild hair, tied back with a scarf. She looked so much like Dora, Lydia felt choked up for a moment, but then the woman spoke again.

"Many layers to a human. Worlds within worlds. Care for a reading?"

"I would, but I'm off somewhere. Are these handmade?" Lydia enquired, looking at an array of exquisitely crafted pieces, spread out on the burgundy colored cloth that covered the table.

The woman smiled, the lines of experience gathering under her grey eyes. "Made by me and the coven," she said winking.

"What is this?" Lydia asked, picking up something with a light-colored handle, carved with runes. It was solid and weighty and felt good in Lydia's hand.

"You've got a good eye. It's an athame, a blade for spells and such," the woman said taking the object from Lydia. She slid a ringed thumb down the seam of the handle and a blade flicked out, locking into place. "For the witch on the go," informed the woman.

"It's beautiful," said Lydia wistfully.

"Carved of bone."

"Human?" Lydia joked. The woman didn't laugh.

"You mustn't repeat the past. You have to change the story. That's the only way to move forward," the woman said straight forwardly.

"You remind me of someone," Lydia said, the corner of her mouth twitching.

"Everyone's just someone who's been here before. None of us are new, just our experiences. At any rate, you have to have this... petal," said the woman, her eyes suddenly lighting up as though someone had just whispered a secret into her ear.

Lydia was taken aback. She stared at the woman for a moment. "How much?"

"No. When the Goddess tells me things, I listen. Take it."

"How can I ever thank you?" Lydia pleaded.

"Don't. It's out of my control," the woman said curiously, before greeting another potential customer.

Lydia looked at her watch and, seeing that she was now late, ran all the way down to the end of the street, reaching back and stuffing the bone-knife into her backpack on the way. Her fitness had improved dramatically since moving further north. Maybe because she was at a loose end with Dean working so prolifically or perhaps it was the feeling that Brianna might stab her in the face one day. Whatever it was, Lydia had become addicted to taking long walks up through Eaton and running alongside the river. The tropical fruit was abundant and Lydia joked that she ate so much of it, she was slowly morphing into a fruit bat. She was faster, stronger and better than ever. In no time at all, Lydia arrived at her destination, barreled in through the automatic doors and signed in at reception just in time to see the rest of the class lining up for Muay Thai.

Chapter Three:

The Seed of the Beast

After class, Lydia showered and changed, guzzling on cold water purchased from the front desk, as she rushed out of the building. She hotfooted it further down the road to a wooden building that looked almost like a taller version of a regular Queenslander-style house, except for the 'Community Center' sign out front. A young, Maori man was tending to the garden in the front yard. He had long black hair and a smattering of stubble on his chin. His eyes were luminescent green, giving him an ethereal look, like he was from a different world. His handsome features lit up as Lydia burst through the front gate.

"Kia Ora, Lydia!" said the young man, rising to his feet.

"Hey there, Porourangi! Replied Lydia.

"I keep telling you, you can call me just: Rangi. We're mates, right?"

"Okay, Rangi," Lydia chuckled.

"Hey, I forgot to tell you, my mum loved that portrait you did of me. I gave it to her for her birthday. She cried and everything."

"I'm really happy to hear that, Rangi. You were a good model."

"I know you're pulling my leg. I get a bit fidgety, eh?"

"Just a bit."

"My dad says I got ants in my pants. I just think I have a lot of energy cos' I'm blessed by Awhiowhio. He's the God of tornadoes!"

"Knowing you these past months, I'd say you're right. All that energy's good for Muay Thai, though. Still remember that sweep-kick I showed you?"

"Course I do," replied Rangi, demonstrating vigorously. "It's good to embrace the blessings, Sis. Choice day, eh?"

"It's a little rippa," said Lydia.

"Nah, don't say rippa. Say 'pai' instead, eh?"

"I enjoy our little Maori lessons. Okay, how's this? It's a pai day then. Did I say that right?" Lydia said with some uncertainty.

Rangi laughed. "Not bad. You'll be talking like a cuz in no time. Chur, Lydia. I gotta' tend to these cordylines," Rangi announced as he dropped to his knees.

Lydia climbed the concrete steps to the center, fanning herself with her hand. She had only just entered when someone slammed into her midsection with considerable force. Lydia hopped to keep her balance before looking down into large, brown eyes.

"Alisi! It's nice to see you too, beautiful," exclaimed Lydia, hugging the ten-year old child.

"How are you, Miss Lydia?" asked Alisi softly.

"I'm good now that I've had a hug from you!"

Alisi pulled away and smiled gleefully at Lydia before running to join the other children in the main hall. There was a stage at the far end and long, thin windows on either side, giving the place a distinctly churchy feel. Easels, canvasses, paints and brushes had been set up in a circle in the middle of the room and twelve children gathered around to use them. Lolani, wearing another of her colorful sarongs, and a hibiscus flower behind her ear, walked over to greet Lydia. Lydia pressed her nose to the other woman's in a traditional Pacific Islander greeting.

"Lolani, half the class is missing. What happened?" Lydia enquired.

"Tangi's parents said he has to do chores at home. Ezekiel's dad says it was his mother that wanted him to learn to paint and now that she's left him, he's going to make Ezekiel get a job. I think that Ngaire is-"

"I get the picture, Lani. It's just that the class gets smaller every week. Soon it'll be just you and me. You're not going to ditch me, are you?" asked Lydia.

"Never," answered Lolani.

"Good. I'd go mad without these classes," added Lydia.

"Is everything okay?" Lolani enquired.

"Everything's great. It's just that Dean has the building and he still crafts pieces from time to time, the odd table and what-have-you, but I still need a creative outlet. I'm not much use when it comes to construction, so art gives me a feeling of purpose, I guess. You know what I mean, Lani. You're a much better artist than I am."

"Oh, that's very kind. I don't get the chance to draw as much as I want to. I have Bertie at home and he needs me. Husbands are like big babies sometimes. But I think art makes me feel like I have a purpose as well."

"Speaking of husbands," added Lydia, thrusting out her hand to show Lani her engagement ring.

"Oh wow, Lydia! Now you're going to have your own big baby!" said Lolani excitedly.

The women embraced after which Lolani grabbed Lydia's hand to take a closer look at her ring finger.

"You're the first person I've told. It feels real now. You like it?" Lydia asked.

"I love it. Dean made this?"

"Yes. He's an artist in his own right."

Lolani beamed at Lydia, but then something like sadness flashed across her face briefly. Lydia knew better than to ask her friend about it; Lolani was one to keep things upbeat.

"Shall we start the class?" Lolani said looking out at the group of children.

The children's heads turned in unison as the sound of heavy boots echoing through the hall caught their attention. A round man with a thick black moustache stormed in, his eyes wide and full of rage.

"Sa evei na bitch?" yelled the man as he picked up a chair and threw it toward the kids, forcing them to scatter.

"Tarova oqo, Bertie!" screamed Lolani, standing in front of the children defensively.

Alisi ran to her side, grabbing at her sarong and burying her face in Lolani's thigh.

Bertie stormed over to Lolani and pulled the child away from her, sending her tiny body skidding across the floor. He then grabbed Lolani by the hair, wrenched her off of her feet and began to drag her across the floor and toward the exit. Some of the children began to cry and Lydia felt a surge of adrenaline, followed by anger. She ran up behind Bertie and propelled a knee into his spine, forcing him to release his hold on Lolani. The rotund man spun around and Lydia wasted no time in delivering a quick jab to his neck followed by an elbow to his nose. Bertie dropped to his knees, wailing like a disgruntled infant. Lydia deftly delivered a kick to Bertie's head and the man fell forward, his bloody face slapping the floor like a raw steak.

Lolani was checking on Alisi as Lydia approached her. The small girl was shaking and sobbing soundlessly and Lolani picked her up and rocked her back and forth. Lydia made eye contact with Lolani, who quickly looked away.

"Lani. He can't do that to you," Lydia insisted.

Lolani turned to look at Lydia, "You made things worse. He's my husband."

DEAN WAS POINTING AND saying something very serious to Ben as Lydia arrived at the building site. Ben had his hands on his hips and he looked more than a little fed up.

"Your lady might be going to jail!" Lydia called out, aiming to defuse the tension.

"What on earth are you talking about?" Dean queried as Ben turned and walked away.

"What's up his butt?" Lydia whispered as she hugged Dean's sweaty torso.

"Never mind him. What have you done?"

"Nothing. Okay, I kicked a guy's ass. He was hurting my friend!" Lydia exclaimed.

Dean shook his head, grinning. "You never fail to surprise me."

"Seriously... you know I can't stand by and watch that happen. Not me. Not after everything."

"I know. You just be careful. Were the cops involved?" Dean enquired.

"The center called them. They questioned me. Said that if he wanted to press charges, well, I don't know." Lydia's voice trailed off.

"They didn't take you downtown?" Dean asked in an ominous tone.

"No."

"Country cops. Maybe they've been called out to the guy's place before. You may be their hero! Maybe you'll make Commissioner one of these days!" Dean quipped.

Lydia slapped Dean's chest. "Sorry, sorry. Don't wanna' make *you* mad."

"You're not sore at me?" Lydia queried.

"No! I'm proud as hell. Bastard sounds like he had it coming."

The sound of squeaky car brakes echoed across the property and Dean looked over to see a taxi pulling up on the street. Lydia squinted and gasped audibly, tugging on Dean's tee shirt as she recognized the person piling out of the vehicle. Lydia jogged toward the visitor, ultimately breaking out into a run. The distant figure followed suit and the pair met in the middle, embracing vigorously.

"Kitty!" cried Lydia.

"Listeria! Damn, woman! You look like an aerobics instructor!" yelled Kitty.

Lydia's smile suddenly faded and she grabbed Kitty by the shoulders. "Wait. What's happening with Mom?"

Kitty's eyes glazed over. "She's gone."

"S-She... but, why didn't y-you call me, text me, anything?" Lydia demanded, stumbling away from her sister.

"I didn't want to tell you over the phone or by text. Mom wouldn't have wanted that. You remember, before she got bad. She'd always insist on a visit. Face to face is-"

"-the only way to communicate like a human being," Lydia continued. "But what about the funeral?"

"Uh... how do I put this," Kitty began furtively. "Mom's with me."

"With you?"

Kitty placed the hat case she was carrying on the ground. She crouched down and undid the zipper, revealing an antique-looking ceramic urn. Kitty carefully pulled the receptacle out of the bag and proffered it to Lydia.

"She's in h-here?"

"Mom specified in her last wishes, that she wanted to be cremated. She also wanted her ashes scattered on Australian soil. You know how she felt about the place," said Kitty, gently caressing the urn.

Lydia suddenly felt numb. Kitty was saying something about home, about Colorado, but Lydia could only hear white noise.

MASON HAD BEEN DENIED pain killers during his hospital stay and he was glad of it. The pain had cleansed him and made him stronger. When Lydia had left him in Colorado for dead, while she escaped to Australia to sleep with every man she could, no doubt, he was enraged. All the while, though, there was a part of him that hoped. He had entertained the idea that he and Lydia would be together in the end. He was a loving man and a patient one. Sure, he disciplined her every now and then, but he always forgave her for making him do that. Lydia was helpless and stupid and he was doing his best to shape her into something better. Now he was experiencing a clarity that had evaded him for their entire relationship. There was no need to forgive her because she was unequivocally evil. 'Evil cannot live' was the phrase that had become Mason's mantra. He had scratched it into the underside of his left forearm with a thumbnail. He stared at his bloody handiwork and laughed when he realized that the word 'live' is just evil backwards. It was a sign from the Gods, the ancient Gods, the ones that were renowned for smiting and punishing and refining mankind with fire.

This was a test. The cell, the bad company, the cramped conditions and the terrible food. Did no one know how to confit an ocean trout filet in this hellhole? The worst thing was the effect on his psychology. Without stimuli, Mason's mind was dulling like a sword without a whetstone. Only a weak soul would register the situation as a complete waste, however. Mason had decided to embrace the place as a sort of training camp. He did a thousand push-ups every other day. He would hold his breath for longer and longer periods, drink his own urine without gagging – that was a valuable skill – and punch the plastered walls to toughen his fists. He was becoming a warrior, a berserker, a beast-man, distilled down into his masculine quintessence.

He had been stretching one night, after his workout, when he heard a voice in the darkness. It was guttural, deep, and it sounded old, not like an old person, but like it was from another time. The voice just called his name at first and it terrified him. But soon, the being, spirit, whatever it was, told him things. It became instructor and sage advisor and above all else: savior. It was from a higher realm, maybe, something reaching its tendrils out to connect with a student of unprecedented potential. The voice growled instructions to Mason and before long, he was filled with confidence in things to come. Everything was happening for a reason, Lydia, his incarceration, everything. The creature was undoubtedly attracted to Mason's strength of body and soul; not just anyone would have been chosen. Most humans were weak and lost and in need of constant reassurance. Not Mason. His Lord and Master saw greatness in him and Mason would not let him down.

Some nights, lying awake, as sleepless inmates paced like hyenas, he would visualize Lydia. He would imagine her floating above him, naked and wet with excitement. She looked like a fresco, or a beautiful Pre-Raphaelite masterpiece. He could smell the gamey perfume of her vagina, he could see her nipples hardening, her tits engorged and eagerly anticipating the heat of his mouth. Her flesh writhed and rippled, every cell reaching out for his dominion. His mouth would open and close rhythmically, like he was a lion, devouring the flesh of a freshly killed zebra. In his more elevated moments, he could taste blood and sweat and fear. When his penis was hard and aching, he would spit in his palm and jerk off until his semen erupted, like a great geyser, in his giant hand. The seed of the Beast.

The remand center echoed with the music of insanity and hopelessness and violence. It smelled like a zoo, but these animals weren't endangered, they were abundant. Society had washed its hands of these miscreants, but Mason saw the truth. The people he was incarcerated with weren't just criminals and they certainly weren't noble savages. They were tools; tools to be used at his discretion. Some of them could manipulate the handlers and source things like alcohol or porn or drugs if one was so inclined. He had yet to find a tool to provide him with a decent drop of red, but that could wait. Some tools had contacts on the outside, the kind that could bully jurors into excluding themselves from selection. If you were big enough and focused enough you could get court proceedings delayed. His new associate, Thomas, was as helpful as they come. Their relationship was mutually beneficial, each man knowing things that would benefit the other. Mason still had money on the outside and Thomas knew people, helpful people. He was rough and uncouth but there was a kind of poetic ugliness to him. Mason made it clear that he was the alpha dog by always looking down at Thomas, never sitting or kneeling in his presence. He wouldn't touch the man, even to shake hands and Mason refused to call him by his street-name: Knuckles. How idiotic. Thomas was a blunt instrument, but effective nevertheless. Mason could feel that his ascension was nigh.

DEAN CARRIED THE HEAVIEST of Kitty's suitcases up the wooden stairs to Brianna's house. He placed the luggage on the floor near the dining table and intercepted his sister in the hallway. There were some whispered words before Brianna rounded Dean to confront Lydia.

"I'm so sorry, Lydia," she said warmly, rubbing Lydia's back.

Faye ran from her room straight up to Kitty. "I'm Faye. What's your name?" she asked excitedly.

"Leave the woman be!" shouted Brianna.

"It's okay. I'm Katherine. You can call me Kitty."

"Meow," replied Faye before leaning backwards and cartwheeling around the table. Captain poked his head out of Faye's bedroom door. He was wearing a bonnet that Faye had imposed on him earlier in the afternoon. The Great Dane exhaled hard, making his jowls undulate, before disappearing back into the room.

"You've met my brother Dean and I'm Brianna, the owner-proprietor of this hostel," Brianna added, looking Kitty up and down.

"Oh look, I'm not here to be a burden. I'm quite happy getting a room in town," blurted Kitty, her ears turning red.

Lydia shot Dean a desperate look and he nodded gravely.

"You should stay the night at least, before you decide what you want to do. You've had a long journey and I'm sure you're exhausted," Dean said, staring into Brianna's eyes and emphasizing the last few words of his offer.

"Why not," Brianna said with exasperation.

"You can sleep in my room, Kitten!" announced Faye.

"Kitty!" corrected Dean shaking his head.

"Come on, I think we should catch up a little bit," asserted Lydia, grabbing Kitty by the arm.

Brianna mumbled something inaudible before retreating to the kitchen. Dean locked eyes with Lydia and Lydia smiled reassuringly at him.

"I need to change," Kitty said, pulling at the fabric of her top.

"You look great. You're probably overdressed for this neck of the woods," Lydia retorted.

Kitty looked at Dean. "She's right," he added.

THE PUB WAS A GOOD thirty-minute walk from Brianna's house and Kitty cursed her high heels. Mosquitoes were out in force and Lydia batted at them casually while Kitty almost toppled over, fanning them away like a crazed hummingbird. The pair arrived at the pub, a long building with a large verandah area upstairs, just in time to witness a drunk man being forcibly removed by the bouncer. The tall bald enforcer picked the man up by the waistband of his sweat pants and literally threw him out onto the street. The drunk guy looked about fifty-years old and had the gin blossomed nose of a seasoned boozer.

"Nice place. We're going to get murdered, aren't we?" said Kitty grimly.

"We'll be fine. I'll protect you, Kitty-Cat," said Lydia confidently.

A couple of younger guys eyed Kitty's legs as she entered the place, her short skirt blown around by the industrial fan running at full power from the side of the bar. An older man removed his fedora and bowed graciously at the two women and Lydia winked at him. One of the young guys jumped off of his stool and jogged over to Kitty and Lydia's side, playfully shouldering Lydia to get her attention. Lydia snapped around, her eyebrows knitted together before a look of surprise washed over her face.

"Rangi!" she howled, slapping the young man on the shoulder.

"Chur Lydia! I never see you in here, eh. Who's your friend?" Rangi queried.

"This is my sister. Her name's Kitty and it's her first time in Australia," Lydia disclosed.

"Haere Mai, Kitty!" said Rangi. "Means: welcome," he added, sensing Kitty's confusion.

"Nice to meet you, Rang-ee," greeted Kitty.

"It's more like: Ruhng-ee. But, not to worry. I've been called worse things. Things I wouldn't repeat in front of a lady," said Rangi, thrusting his hands deep into the pockets of his jeans.

"Rangi takes care of the Community Center grounds, where I work," offered Lydia.

"Yeah but I don't take care of business as good as you, Lydia. You really handed Bertie's ass to him. That boy deserved a belting. Would've given it to him myself, if I had half the chance," said Rangi, affecting a fighting pose.

"What's this all about?" Kitty enquired.

"Nothing. Just a scuffle earlier today," Lydia mumbled.

"Don't sell yourself short, Killer. You were ace!" Rangi bubbled.

"Listen, Rangi, my sister and I-" began Lydia.

"-would like to invite you to have a drink with us," Kitty interjected.

Rangi looked at Lydia who simply shrugged at him. "It would be my esteemed honor, my good woman-folks," said Rangi, holding out his arm.

Kitty took hold of Rangi's arm and beamed at her sister, who looked down and smiled to herself.

Several drinks later, the party of three were conversing animatedly. The table was littered with empty martini glasses and several half-finished jugs of concoctions containing coconut cream and pineapple juice. There were shot-glasses and wedges of lime, little umbrellas and slices of fruit everywhere. Kitty was in interviewer mode, intent on garnering all possible details of Rangi's homeland. Every fact he divulged about the place was 'fascinating' or 'magnificent' to her. Lydia rolled her eyes when Kitty said that she could see herself packing up and moving to New Zealand. Kitty had progressively moved closer and closer to the young man over the course of the evening, until she was almost in his lap. She had pulled her ponytail out and was busy teasing her brown locks coquettishly. Lydia hadn't even seen her undo the buttons at her neckline, but there was definitely plenty to see every time she laughed or leant forward. Rangi was gentlemanly enough not to stare, at least not in Lydia's presence. The young man kept looking into Lydia's face, as though he were waiting on approval, or permission to show interest. Either way, it was clear that Kitty was attracted to Rangi. Kitty had a good six years on him at least, as the man hadn't cleared his twenties yet.

"I think it's time to go, Kitty," announced Lydia, standing up unsteadily.

"I'm gonna' stay," Kitty slurred.

"I'll take care of her," Rangi interjected.

"Thanks, Rangi, but-" Lydia began.

"I'm not a baby!" Kitty spat.

"Listen, in light of everything. I really think it's time we go," Lydia added sternly.

"You're not Mom!" Kitty shot back, tears welling in her eyes.

Rangi looked back and forth between the two women, slightly baffled. Kitty stood up and ran to the bathroom and Lydia followed her.

Kitty pushed the door open with such force that it banged against the wall and hit her in the shoulder. She stumbled over to one of the sinks and washed her face. Lydia sidled up to her and looked at her sister's reflection in the bathroom's long mirror.

"You're drunk, Kitty. You've been hitting the booze hard tonight and I get it. It's okay. We both have to deal with Mom's death in our own way," Lydia said, rubbing Kitty's back.

"Death? You're so harsh," said Kitty.

"What should I say?" Lydia queried.

Kitty stared at her own reflection. "I don't know. Passing? It's not real, is it? She'll still be there when I get home," Kitty said softly as she slumped against the vanity.

"I know I should say something lame, like: 'we can keep her alive by remembering her'. I don't have it in me, though. We loved her and she loved us. We still love her. That's all."

Kitty fell against Lydia and her sister embraced her.

"Get a room!" shouted a passing teenager, leaving the stall without washing her hands.

"What did you say, bitch-face?" countered Lydia, lunging at the girl.

"Stop! What are you doing?" Kitty protested, holding Lydia back.

"Yeah, keep moving!" Lydia added as the teenager skittered for the bathroom door.

"What's happening to you?" Kitty begged.

"What?" Lydia shot back.

"I'm hanging out with Rangi. He's nice and... calm," Kitty stated, backing away from her sister.

"You know what? Just go." Lydia sneered.

LYDIA WAS SLUMPED UNDER the clothesline in Brianna's backyard, cradling the half empty bourbon bottle she'd bought on the way home. The early morning air was crisp and fresh and the chorus of birds that Lydia normally enjoyed, irritated her. Even Captain knew well enough to leave her alone, retreating to his favorite spot under the house, where he chewed on a pig's ear. Lydia's head spun every time she closed her eyes, so she resigned herself to staring up into the sky. The moon was still vaguely visible, a half-eaten cantaloupe wedge hanging in the heavens. Brianna emerged from the house at one point, muttering something about Lydia not letting Faye see her in her drunken state. Lydia could barely absorb anything happening around her and she didn't want to. At that moment, she wished that she could just sink into the lawn, never to be seen again. There was a dull pain that accosted her entire body, no, it was deeper than that, her soul was in agony.

Lydia took a long drink from her bottle and stifled a retch. She tried to stand but fell right back down again, like a baby attempting its first steps. Captain made a whining noise through his nose and Lydia mimicked him before laughing to herself manically. She tried to stand again, but this time she floated up onto her own two feet with no effort at all. Lydia smiled at her grace and poise and looked down to admire her efforts, but there were two large feet beside her own. She was confused as she was certain she only had two feet, last time she'd checked. Lydia giggled and stomped the feet she was familiar with to see if the newly discovered ones would do the same. They didn't.

"Come on. Let's get you inside," Dean said gently as he propped Lydia up and turned her toward the back door.

"Oh, it's the love of my life! Here, 'ave a drink, sweetheart," Lydia offered loudly, thrusting the bottle at Dean.

"I'm fine. Better give me that, for keeps, lady," Dean said, prizing the bourbon bottle from Lydia's hand.

"Yeah, fair enough. Let's have some sex," Lydia suggested jovially.

Dean laughed and walked Lydia toward the house. "Let's see how things go, eh?" Dean suggested patiently.

"You know, you got some lovely eyes, you-" Lydia was interrupted by a stream of vomit that poured out of her in almost a perfect arc.

"That's it, get it all out," Dean encouraged.

Lydia wiped at her mouth and stared at the puddle on the grass in front of her. "Is that mine?" she asked, as though she had just awoken from a long sleep.

"It belongs to Captain now," Dean quipped.

Brianna appeared at the door and waved Dean and Lydia indoors.

"Come on, quickly! For pity's sake! It's not helping things, behaving like this!" Brianna chided.

"Give her a break. She's just had the worst news of her life!" Dean scolded. Brianna stormed off into the early morning shadows.

LYDIA AWOKE IN THE late afternoon to Dean dabbing at her forehead with a damp washcloth. He smiled at her and helped her sit up, placing pillows behind her lower back. He put a glass of something cold and fizzy to Lydia's lips, taking it away when she'd had enough. Lydia looked around the room, spotting a bucket next to the bed that had been clearly emptied and cleaned recently, as there were traces of soap suds in the channel at the bottom. Something on the far side of the bedroom caught Lydia's eye, something reflective and round. It was the urn containing her mom's ashes, but it was sitting atop a wooden plinth, carved with beautiful Celtic-looking shapes.

"Do you like it? I made it last night. The base is oak, nice and strong, and the top is walnut," Dean explained.

Lydia buried her face in Dean's chest and he wrapped his arms around her. Pulling away and looking into Dean's dark eyes, Lydia felt a surge of passion for the man.

"It's perfect," Lydia gushed, her voice thinning out into a near squeak at the end.

"Good," Dean said happily.

"Oh, I have something for you. Can you pass me my backpack?" Lydia requested.

Dean returned with the bag and handed it to Lydia. She pulled the pack open and pulled out a weighty object. She looked at the thing, running a finger down its side, before flipping it over and repeating the motion. A blade snapped open, fixing in place, and Lydia, startled, dropped the knife, laughing.

"There you go. It's a witches' blade. But it was so gorgeously made, I thought of you and your crafty hands. Also, a badass needs a cool knife."

"Wow! I really dig it. Thanks, lady," Dean said appreciatively, studying the object, then kissing Lydia's head.

"You're very welcome."

"Can I get you anything? Are you hungry?" Dean offered.

"Oh no. Not yet, thank you. Did... Kitty come back last night?" Lydia enquired.

"No. I don't think so. What happened?"

"She stayed at the pub. She was hanging out with a guy I know. He's a good guy but I hope she's okay."

Lydia reached for her handbag on the bedside table. She pulled out her phone and checked her messages. There was a message from Kitty with an attached photo of her and Rangi smiling and smooshing their faces together. Lydia smiled and then exhaled with some relief. Then the color suddenly drained from Lydia's face and she reached for the bucket beside the bed.

CAPTAIN'S BREATH SMELLED of meat and Lydia fought off a wave of nausea as the dog licked her face. The room was dark and Lydia sat bolt upright when she realized she'd slept until nightfall. Captain barked and Lydia stroked his head as she spilled out of bed. The muffled sound of television and utensils scraping across plates emanated through the bedroom walls. Lydia glanced at the beautiful plinth Dean had made for her mother's urn and she smiled to herself. Lydia pictured Dean's face as she changed her clothes and she wondered if he was eating with his sister and niece. The sound of footsteps crunching on the gravel outside the window caught Lydia's attention. More often than not, strange outdoor sounds could be blamed on Captain, but he was in the room. The dog cocked one ear and stared at the window for a second, but opted to lick himself rather than investigate further. Lydia was happy to be too tired to care. Whatever it was, it could amuse itself until Lydia had eaten. She wasn't the scared little waif of years gone by; she was evolving. Lydia smoothed out her hair and meandered out the bedroom door and down the hall to the dining area. Dean was indeed seated at the table with Brianna, but Faye was not with them.

"No Faye?" Lydia questioned.

"She's at a friend's house. Don't want her around drunkenness and carry-on like that," Brianna said curtly.

"Calm down, Bri," Dean retorted. "Food time?"

"Yes please," Lydia responded vigorously, realizing how hungry she now was.

"Coming right up. Take a seat," Dean said with a wink, disappearing into the kitchen to fetch dinner for Lydia.

Lydia sheepishly sat at the table, opposite Brianna who glowered at her the whole time. Brianna finally dropped her gaze to Lydia's left hand, as it smoothed out the tablecloth.

"Congratulations," Brianna said awkwardly, suddenly looking at the TV.

"Thank you. You know, Brianna, I really appreciate you letting me stay while the house is being built. I just wanted to say that, again. I'm really grateful," Lydia said without taking a breath.

Brianna looked back at Lydia, as though she were scanning her comments for sincerity.

"Well... you're welcome."

Brianna looked up at the ceiling, her jaw clenched shut. She dropped her head, then lifted it again, shifting in her seat as though she couldn't get comfortable. Lydia furtively looked at Brianna, fidgeting like Faye did when she wanted to leave the table and play with the dog. She wondered whether the woman was suppressing the desire to throw something, when Brianna spoke again.

"I really am sorry about your mum. Family's all there is in the end. D will always see you right. He's a good man. That may sound like an insipid compliment, but it's not. There's a shortage of really good men, I know that for a fact. Faye's father was an okay person. He tried, I suppose. He wasn't *good*, though. Faye was a sick kid. She used to have seizures. First sign of hardship, he pissed off to Norfolk Island to manage a hotel or some damn thing. D won't do that to you," Brianna said, in a harsh staccato that sounded like someone reading out a cake recipe aloud.

Dean returned with a plate of lamb chops and vegetables. Brianna nodded emphatically to herself and left the table.

"Everything okay?" Dean asked, looking back at Brianna as she disappeared down the corridor.

"Really good, I think," Lydia responded, before attacking the food on her plate like Captain with a bone.

Chapter Four:

Breaching the Surface

Lydia retired early, still feeling a little under the weather and Dean, feeling restless, decided to give his brand new, second-hand bike a run. Dean walked the bike out of Brianna's external garage and hopped on when he reached the street. He started up the motorcycle and smiled at the sound of the engine, revving it just to hear it growl. Dean took off away from the house and headed in the direction of Flying Fish Point. Faye had nagged him relentlessly about taking her to see the flying fish, that really jumped more than flew. Everything had taken a backseat to the house being built and now Ben had 'spat the dummy', taking off for who-knows how long. At least things seemed to be getting better with Brianna and Lydia; the house had been extremely tense of late.

Dean accelerated, enjoying the wind in his hair. He realized that he hadn't had more than a moment to himself for some time. It felt good to be alone with his thoughts. All those years with the gang had forced him to think in terms of what was good for the group. Now he was free to think of what was good for himself, and more importantly, Lydia. Taking a step back and admiring his new life was something of a novelty. Soon he would have a home, a real home. He never knew that he wanted one until he was confronted with the possibility. It was all so clear now: the gang was a placeholder for what he really needed. Life was still about courage and honor and loyalty, but to a single person, and in the future, hopefully more than that. Things with the Wild

Colonial Boys hadn't ended well and it was then, that Dean clearly saw that he had made the right call by taking his leave.

Gusty winds buffeted Dean's bike as he hurtled across the river toward the coast. There were palm fronds on the road along with the usual flattened cane-toads. The storm season was imminent and along with the usual fear and caution, there was something else. There was something in the air, something electric. Meteorologists would probably chalk it up to something in the ionosphere, but whatever it was, it was a rush. Part of Dean wanted to throw Lydia on the back of the bike and keep on riding forever. When they had first set off for the far north, albeit under tragic circumstances, there was something intoxicating about it. The idea of starting again, hitting the reset button on everything and reshaping their life together, it was like a drug. Of course, the feeling had subsided and life pushed on like it always does. Either way, as long as he had Lydia, he was happy. Suddenly, Dean's meditations were intruded on by the feeling that he was no longer alone.

The distant roar of approaching bike engines had Dean on edge. In the old days, that sound meant that something bad was about to go down. Any gang that wasn't yours, was a potential threat. Dean knew better than to change direction or speed, he just checked his mirrors intently to identify who he was dealing with. His heart sank when he identified the emblem of The Eternal Vampyres: a club affiliated with The Wild Colonial Boys. The two Motorcycle Clubs had shared interests once upon a time and that relationship still held water. There were only three riders, not the entire MC, which was a small victory in itself. Dean had the nagging feeling he'd seen one of them before, but he couldn't place where. If they recognized him, there'd be questions to answer. Dean threw caution to the wind and sped up.

Checking his mirrors, it appeared that the bikers weren't interested in him after all. He had put a good distance between himself and them but they didn't give chase. Dean was relieved to see the small crew turn off at the next T-junction. Dean took the next left whilst cautiously surveying the area. He was almost at the water when he heard the familiar sound of bikes, approaching from his right flank. The bikers were moving at full pelt and Dean took off rapidly, his pursuers closing in. Zig-zagging through back streets wherever he could, he couldn't shake the trio. There was no way he was going to head home or anywhere near it, he wasn't about to play into their hands. Emerging onto Jubilee Road, he decided he would lead them through the forest at Jubilee Heights. Dean checked his fuel gage and realized that he didn't have a lot of fuel left. Maybe he could ditch his bike and head into the trees on foot. When they caught up with him, there'd be hell to pay, but at least they'd be far away from Bri's house and far away from Lydia.

Twisting the throttle, Dean negotiated the curves of the road gracefully but the bikers gained on him on the straights. Deciding that it was now or never, Dean skidded to a halt. He was just about to disappear into the bush, when the biker at the head of the pack pulled something from inside his leather jacket. Dean ducked behind his bike as the muffled sound of a silenced gunshot confirmed Dean's suspicions. To Dean's surprise, the crew roared past without stopping, the last biker to pass, hurled something large at Dean as he peered up over his bike saddle. The thing whizzed past Dean's ear and tumbled into the shrubs on the side of the road. Something caught Dean's eye as the object was thrown; it was the missing index finger and the tattoo just behind the knuckle. The biker who threw the object was someone Dean knew, or at least knew of. He racked his brain, but he could only see vague fragments of who that hand might belong to. Dean watched the bikes disappear, half expecting them to turn around and come at him again. Dean rounded his bike to look for the point of the bullet's impact and soon spotted his deflating rear tire with a perfect hole in it. Dean's mind raced and he ran over to find the object that had hurtled past his head. Pushing through the bushes, he finally discovered a hessian sack and the hairs on the back of his neck stood up as he noticed the bottom of the bag was soaked in blood.

Dean closed his eyes and inhaled before picking up the bag and looking inside. At first, Dean wasn't sure what he was looking at. He tipped the bag's contents onto the dirt and his heart began to thump as he locked eyes on the face he knew so well. It was the severed head of their dog: Captain. Dean felt dizzy with horror and outrage. He sunk to his knees, cradling the animal's head like an infant.

"I'm so sorry, boy," he whispered.

He placed the dog's head on the ground gently, tears in his eyes. Dean stood up as the realization hit him: this diversion was working. Dean took one last look at Captain, before running down the road. He focused all of his will on spotting passing cars; they had been few and far between on the way up. Dean ran at full speed toward the next intersection, anger and fear pushing him harder and harder. Finally, a large four-wheel drive barreled down the road past Dean as he waved frantically at it. Dean felt the sinking sensation that the driver was going to ignore him, but the glow of brake lights signaled a win. Dean climbed in and urged the driver to take him home as fast as possible. He pulled his wallet from his jeans pocket but the older female driver told him to put it away. Dean recognized her as a lady who worked in town, at one of the mixed-business stores. She rattled on about seeing him around the place recently but Dean could only answer in monosyllables. He could only think about what was possibly happening in his absence. He'd heard of the price paid by brothers leaving an MC. Often it wasn't just a price exacted on the offender, it was their family that suffered too. Finally, after what felt like an eternity, they pulled up outside Brianna's house.

Dean thanked the older lady and flew out of the passenger side door and up the stairs. There was no activity inside and Dean searched every room, until Brianna emerged, looking half asleep. Dean hugged her, before ignoring her enquiries and flying into the guest bedroom. The bedclothes were disturbed but Lydia wasn't there.

"Where did she go?" Dean demanded.

"I don't know. Out for a drink, maybe?" Brianna offered feebly. "Why the panic?"

"Lock the doors. Don't answer if anyone knocks." Dean instructed.

"What is this, D? You're scaring me."

"You need to be scared," Dean added, before heading out the back door.

Captain's body was laying under the clothesline, a pool of blood under his neck. Dean steeled himself and clenched his fists. He ran up the side of the house looking for signs of a struggle. There was nothing, she must have been taken silently and quickly. Feeling hopeless, he returned to his and Lydia's room for another look. He tore the room apart but there was nothing. Helplessness began to wash over him and Dean sat on the bed, racking his brain for answers. He could hear Brianna shuffling around in the distance and he hopped up and closed the bedroom door, craving silence. That's when he saw it: a note with a belt-buckle blade jammed into it, fastening it to the door. He got up and walked over slowly, fearing what he might discover. The childish writing stated: 'Your woman's waiting for you at home'. Dean felt cold in the small of his back but his face was hot. How could this be happening? He thought they'd been careful. Dean pulled himself together and bolted to his pickup, flinging himself into the driver's seat. He turned the key and realized that If the gang was onto him, they must have been watching for some time. The guy at Mission Beach was no coincidence. His blood boiled as he imagined some scumbag watching his sister, his niece and worst of all: Lydia. Dean sped off for the building site, the blood of his dead dog drying into a crust on his fingers.

THE FIREPLACE CRACKLED and Lydia sat, curled up with a mug of cocoa, on the floor with Kitty. Ulysses purred and rubbed up against her, ignoring Kitty's invitation to sit in her lap. The icy winds outside, rattled the windows and shook the front door, but the sanctuary of the fire made it all irrelevant. Lydia's marshmallows had melted into a pink island in the middle of the chocolate sea in her giant mug. Kitty begged her for a sip, but Lydia refused because she had a cold, Kitty seemed to sniff her way right through winter every year. Soon they would sit down to roast turkey and sweet potatoes and it would be peaceful because Dad was sick in bed. There would be no one to tell them not to talk at the dinner table, or to not blow bubbles in their milk. They would get through an entire evening without feeling the sting of Dad's belt for one or more dinnertime transgressions. The fire spat and hissed and Lydia moved back as the smell of smoke got stronger. Was the chimney blocked?

Lydia's eyes had trouble focusing and her mouth felt all wrong. Her left arm felt numb and her head throbbed, hard. She could see the flicker of flames and she tried to cry out, but there was cloth in her mouth. Her arm was numb, it seemed, because she was laying on it, on the floor. Her arms and ankles were zip-tied behind her and her wrists ached. Lydia wriggled and did her best to move away from the fire but she soon realized that the entire house frame was ablaze. Lydia knew then that she was trapped and she had the sickly, sinking sensation that this would be her end. All she could think about, was Dean. They would never live together in this house and she would never be Lydia Connors. What about Kitty? Kitty would feel so alone. Lydia wondered at the sudden onset of calmness she felt, a feeling that defeated everything else. Calmness mixed with sadness. The smoke made her feel light-headed and sort of high. She could even see Dean's face, hovering above her own. He looked panicked but determined and strong, always so strong. Lydia gave in to the fantasy of Dean picking her up and heroically running through a wall of flame with her body thrown over his shoulder. Then she passed out.

DORA FLOATED ABOVE Lydia, her clothing billowing and flickering like flames around her body. Her eyes were sunken and her cheekbones protruded like blades that threatened to pierce her pale skin. Her lips were thin and they had receded to expose her gums and rotting teeth. She looked more like a corpse now, as if she'd been busily decomposing since her last appearance, but she was somehow able to move and speak. Dora's breath rattled out of her; the sound of it was like the very portent of death and rot.

"Evil's withered hand feels about for you. I will do what I can," said Dora in a thin, raspy voice.

Lydia wanted to cry out, but she couldn't. The thing that spoke didn't look like her friend. The sound of gale-force winds suddenly drowned out the thing's labored breathing. The corpse's head creakily turned away and a sudden gust blew it's remains into countless fragments. Lydia wanted nothing more than to run away, but she couldn't. Lydia soon became painfully aware of the restraints that secured her arms and legs but the wind quickly died down. The tempest was replaced with the crackling of fire; a great blaze that devoured the air and swirled around Lydia like some living thing.

THE HOSPITAL ROOM SMELLED like chemicals and the lights were too bright. Something intrusive was in Lydia's nostrils and her head was bandaged. Her chest hurt with every breath and her temples pulsated. There was a hand gripping Lydia's and she looked over, expecting to see Dean, but was met with Kitty's soft features instead.

"I was so worried about you!" Kitty gushed.

"Yeah, are you gonna' be okay, Sis?" enquired Rangi, looming up from behind Kitty.

"I'm okay. Where's Dean?"

"Cops were asking questions, so I told him to disappear. He seems like the kind of guy that shouldn't be questioned, am I right?"

"What happened?" Lydia asked groggily.

"Someone whacked you on the head. Took you to the building site. Oh God, Lydia. I'm sorry I wasn't there," Kitty sobbed. Rangi wrapped a consoling arm around Kitty's shoulders.

"It's not your fault. Where is Dean?"

"Back at his sister's, maybe? He called me on your phone. I spoke to the cops. Told them there was some dispute over your land. They seemed to buy it."

"Look at you, Cuz. Evading the law, like Ned Kelly and stuff. What a romantic lifestyle you got, Lydia. I'm all jealous, and that, eh," Rangi enthused, his arms flailing about.

"Rangi, can we have a sister to sister moment, please?" Lydia implored.

"You got it, girl. Chur ladies," Rangi said cheerily as he exited the room.

Lydia waited until Rangi had disappeared before speaking again. "It was Mason, wasn't it?"

Kitty rubbed her wrist and looked at the linoleum floor. "He's in prison though, right?"

"Remand. Same thing, I guess. He's awaiting trial, or so I thought."

"Is there anyone else who might have done something like this?"

"No. I don't think so. I'm not real popular, but..."

"What do you mean?"

"Well, there's the flirty Ukrainian who'd love to wrap her iron thighs around Dean. Brianna hates me, or hated me at least. She's not insane enough to try to burn me to death... I don't think. Then there's the guy I kicked in the face," Lydia thought out loud as she propped herself up in bed.

"The guy Rangi was talking about the other night?"

"Yeah. If it's not Mason, then it could be him. I can't say for sure."

"I'm worried about you, Lydia. I mean, I always worry, but I'm really worried now."

"Don't worry about me. I'm ready for whatever it is," Lydia said with one eyebrow cocked.

"Don't say that. None of us is ever really ready for the bad stuff," responded Kitty.

"Especially if it comes in threes," Lydia said in almost a whisper, looking out the window.

"Huh?"

"Nothing. So, you're still staying with Rangi?" Lydia queried, changing the subject.

"Yeah. He's... unspoiled. You know what I mean? I've never met anyone like him. Nothing seems to get him down. It's like he wouldn't know *how* to be bitter about life. He makes me smile," Kitty said with a far-off look.

"I'm happy to hear that. I want the best for you."

Lydia was suddenly distracted by a long, dark shape that now invaded her peripheral vision. She slowly turned her head and laid eyes on a man in his forties, with long hair tied up in a ponytail. His skin was scarred with pock-marks and his nose was crooked, like it had been broken at least once or twice. His bushy handlebar moustache made him look like an extra in a B-grade film from the seventies. He wore a leather vest with silver skull buttons and his arms were covered in tattoos of skeletons, snakes and naked women. The man sipped from a paper cup and he appeared to be staring at Lydia, though she couldn't be sure due to his dark, wraparound sunglasses. Lydia stared back at the stranger defiantly, resentful of the idea that she was meant to be intimidated. Then as suddenly as he had appeared, the man was gone.

Lydia looked at Kitty and Kitty glared back at her, with an expression of disquiet.

"Ms. Hawkins?" enquired a tall woman, materializing in the doorway, her ginger hair pulled back tight. She was wearing a gunmetal colored pants suit and brandishing a shiny badge.

"Yes?" replied Lydia, still scanning the doorway from time to time for any sign of the biker-looking guy.

"Detectives Crowe and Lee. Can we have a quick word?" queried Detective Crowe, entering the room before receiving a response.

"Why not."

Kitty looked at the detectives and then back at Lydia. "You're going to be okay?" she asked.

"You go. I'll be fine," answered Lydia, adjusting herself.

The hefty woman took a seat and motioned for her partner to do the same. The male was a foot shorter than Crowe and much skinnier.

"You're okay to talk, after everything that happened?"

"Let's just get it over with, huh?" Lydia urged impatiently.

"Right you are. We're having trouble piecing things together. Your sister told us something about an issue with the land you're building on... who is it that's doing the build for you?"

"Oh, friend of the family. Is that really important?"

"Well, it might be. You must have a suspect in mind, then," prodded Detective Crowe.

"Look, not really. Kitty might have exaggerated a little. I really don't know who did this. There are some real nutcases out there. You know what I'm talking about," Lydia prattled as she poured herself a cup of water from a plastic jug.

"Sure. You're a long way from home, aren't you?"

"Look, the house is going to be an investment. My visa is in order. I've done nothing wrong," Lydia lied.

"Hell of an altercation at the Community Center the other day. I wasn't there, but I heard about it. Officer Thompson's a good bloke... little lenient..." Detective Crowe's voice trailed off.

"Are you here to arrest me? Is that it?"

"Calm down. No one's arresting anyone just yet. Should we?" chuckled the female detective.

"I'm glad you find this amusing, Detective."

"You gotta' laugh now and then. It's that or go bloody troppo. You're here alone? I mean, there's no boyfriend... girlfriend?"

"No."

"That's a nice ring. Wood is it? Never seen one like that bef-"

"It was my mother's. She's dead! Okay?" interrupted Lydia, her ears turning red.

"Alright. We're not here to upset you. Take this card. If you think of anything that may help us nut this one out, you call okay?"

Crowe handed Lydia a card featuring her cell phone number and an email address. The large woman nodded as she and her partner ambled out of the room, lingering as though they were trying to absorb every last detail they could. Lydia slumped over and sighed heavily, relieved but still agitated. She didn't doubt for a moment that they knew all about her and Dean and possibly even what happened back in Surfer's Paradise. They would probably just wait for the opportune time and then it would all be over. Lydia imagined what jail would be like. She'd be glad of her fighting skills on the inside. Would she be somebody's bitch? Maybe she was tough enough now to make someone else *her* bitch? Lydia laughed grimly.

"You wanna' get outta' here?"

Lydia turned to look at the door, unsure of who to expect next. It was Brianna, with Faye in tow, beckoning resolutely. Faye charged in and jumped on the end of the bed.

"Uncle Dean said we have to take you home!" Faye gushed excitedly.

"Shhhh!" hissed Brianna.

Lydia wasted no time in getting herself organized. As soon as she was ready, she sidled up to Brianna. Faye vaulted off the bed and ran over to Lydia, bouncing and chattering.

"We're just gonna' walk out. Okay," ordered Brianna.

"We can do that?" Lydia queried.

"They're so understaffed, they won't notice if we're confident about it," replied Brianna.

"Okay, if you're sure," Lydia added.

"Trust me. I used to clean this bloody place. Let's go!" Brianna snapped.

The trio left the room without delay, turning one corner, then another. A Doctor approached with a finger extended upward, as if he intended to say something. Brianna motioned for the party to change direction and head down a long hallway, with a brightly colored sign at the end that said: 'Pediatrics'. They brushed past a clump of helium balloons with giraffes on them, turned left, then left again and jogged down some stairs before emerging into the sunlight. Brianna gave Lydia a push and pulled Faye by the hand and in no time, they were at Dean's pickup. Dean was hunched over in the driver's seat wearing his cowboy hat, pulled down low, and he waved the three females inside. Lydia climbed into the seat beside Dean as Faye and Brianna piled into the back. Dean wrapped a rough hand around the back of Lydia's neck and pulled her in for a kiss. As Lydia's lips met Dean's, she could sense his relief.

"I like the gown," Dean quipped. "Could be fun."

Lydia laughed huskily and Dean stared into her eyes for a moment, before starting up the vehicle and heading for home.

KNUCKLES HAD COME THROUGH for Mason, hooking him up with a cell phone with practiced ease. Security was tighter in the

Southport Remand Center than Mason had anticipated. He'd half expected to be holed up in a tin shed when they'd moved him from hospital to his place of halfway incarceration. Australia was really just a glorified penal colony, as far as he was concerned. That's why his associate: Thomas aka Knuckles, was so good at sourcing things on request, it was in his DNA. Thomas had also very efficiently provided Mason with a steady supply of oats, something that most other inmates had little access to. The high protein and calorific profile in porridge turned out to be ideal for piling on slabs of muscle. Mason focused on his goals while he completed his last set of push-ups. Drops of sweat dotted the concrete floor and he could feel the veins in his neck bulging. He visualized the testosterone surging through his system, making him bigger and stronger and scarier. Maybe it was the concentration of masculine energy that made inmates stack on muscle mass on the inside, then again, maybe it was all the smuggled steroids and supplements. Either way, Mason felt like he could easily tear a man's head clean off, if ever the need arose.

Mason completed his final rep with a growl, before rising to his knees. He took a deep breath and closed his eyes, meditatively. He enjoyed the sweat trickling in rivulets down the channel of his spine. He enjoyed the pumped feeling in his arms, shoulders and chest. He enjoyed the image of tearing Lydia and her stupid boyfriend in half with his bare hands. Jumping to his feet in one fluid motion, Mason skulked over to his bed, looking around all the while. He pulled up the mattress and retrieved his new phone, scanning his text messages. There was a new one from his contact, the one Knuckles had established for him, through the Eternal Vampyres biker club. The message was plain: the contact who had found Lydia and Dean, had finally made a move. It was as Mason feared though, they had tried to kill Lydia. They intended on taking vengeance for Dean turning his back on The Wild Colonial Boys MC, but he'd made it clear that he wanted to get his hands on his lost little lamb. It was all amounting to a conflict of interests and it was becoming a big old mess. All he wanted to know was where Lydia had ended up. He told his contact that he could do what he wanted to Dean.

Mason had to get out of his concrete box, and soon. He knew that he could manifest his escape if he just concentrated hard enough. He was getting so strong that perhaps he would soon be able to just punch a hole in the wall and walk out. This was no place for a Beast-God. Mason shot a glance at his phone once more, he wanted to re-read the message before stowing it away in its hiding place. The words made him seethe. He had to resist the urge to smash the stupid device against the wall. Lydia was in hospital, having narrowly escaped death. In the end, she was used as a warning, but what if they'd killed her by mistake? Would she and this Dean idiot just move on to some other town now? Surely Thomas's biker network had its limits. Ben would just have to try and keep them both there. He had already invested a lot of time in observing the two of them, befriending them, even working for them. Him and his cousin, Debbie. Between the two of them, they had been watching the building site and the sister's house constantly. Apparently, this Debbie character was something of an actress; hopefully she wasn't a crappy one or the whole thing would be blown to pieces.

Mason texted his new orders to Ben and then hid the phone again. He had just lowered the mattress and spun around to sit on it, when the warden told him he had a visitor. Mason shrugged as the screw disappeared and a suited man replaced him at the cell entrance. The man was Mason's legal counsel and he had news.

Chapter Five:

Prey

Dean held Lydia close before Captain's burial site in Brianna's backyard, just under a Paw Paw tree. Faye had cried so much at seeing the dog's grave, Brianna decided to drag her indoors. The moon was the color of bone and almost full. A gust of wind made the banana leaves rustle and nocturnal things sang mournfully. Dean and Lydia stood there wordlessly, there was nothing to say. After a time, the rear screen-door creaked open then slapped shut. Grass crunched as Brianna approached the pair from behind.

"I'm sorry about Captain. He was a good dog," Brianna said, rubbing her hands down the front of her dress as though she had just completed a grimy task.

"Yes, he was," Dean responded sadly.

"Just heard on the news, that there's a cyclone headed our way. They bloody insist on going back to naming them after women," Brianna mumbled, smoothing out her hair.

"Why, what's this one called?" Lydia asked.

"Cyclone Dora. Can you believe that?"

Lydia and Dean looked at one another, dumbfounded.

Dean then watched his sister fidgeting with the buttons on her cuffs. "What is it?" he asked.

"I'm not one to beat around the bush. You know me. After everything that's happened, it's best that Faye and me distance ourselves from all the trouble that's coming. It's not over, whatever it is. I've gotta look-"

"I know," Dean interjected.

"Where will you go?" Lydia asked.

"Actually, I thought it was time that you and D find somewhere to move on to," Brianna added, looking down at her feet, a little embarrassed.

"No. It's time I was straight with you. Both of you. Back in Surfer's, when I split from the MC, there was some trouble," Dean began.

"Yeah, you got shot," Lydia stated.

"Yeah, but there was something else. I didn't want to add to your problems at the time, but I ran into one of the guys I from the club, a bloke we called Knuckles."

"Knuckles? Oh, that can't be good," Brianna exclaimed.

"Well, he suggested I come back. He suggested it hard. He threatened me, and he made a threat aimed squarely at you, Lydia," Dean said solemnly.

"But... how did he even know about me? Jesus, they were watching, weren't they? They're always watching," Lydia said, with an air of dread.

"I saw some members of a gang based up here. They've run with my old crew in the past and they kept me distracted long enough to... do what they did to you."

"This is out of control!" Brianna barked. "I'm not having my daughter, your niece, wrapped up in this, D!"

"What up, beautiful people!" called Rangi, appearing from the side of the house, gripping Kitty's hand.

"We came back to look for you, Lydia, but they said you'd left without being discharged?" Kitty said incredulously. "I've got to pick up my stuff, anyway."

"Never mind that now! You'd be better off heading back the way you came!" Brianna shot back at Kitty.

Kitty blinked and her expression was that of a child, who had just been spanked unexpectedly.

"No, wait. This could work out for the best. Rangi, you wouldn't happen to have some spare room at your place, would you?" Lydia implored.

"For you, Big Sis? 'Course I do!" answered Rangi brightly.

Lydia wanted to hug the boy in that moment. "Could Brianna and her daughter stay at your place for a while? I know it's a lot to ask. We wouldn't ask if things weren't so... bad."

"Hey, I understand. My Uncle Derek used to stay with us until 'things blew over' all the time. He's in prison now though," Rangi said earnestly.

"Rangi!" Kitty chided.

"Oh, don't worry. He's out on parole soon. Also, I don't think you guys will go to prison," Rangi added quickly.

"You going to be all set for the storm?" Dean asked Rangi.

"Yeah, bro. We'll batten down them hatches, eh," Rangi said in his sing-song voice.

Brianna looked at Dean pleadingly and Dean nodded at her, gesturing for her to head inside and get organized. Brianna wheeled around and marched for the back door, but not before shooting an accusatory glance at Lydia.

Lydia threw her hands up in the air, "This is my fault, too?"

Kitty and Rangi followed Brianna into the house and Dean folded his arms across his chest, turning to look out at the night sky. Lydia played with her engagement ring, spinning it around on her ring finger over and over again. A part of her, hunched up and terrified in the back somewhere, wanted to run. Lydia played out the possibility of leaving everything and everyone behind. She had always known that Dean had a past, but he hadn't been entirely honest about the threat that had been looming over both of them all this time. Try as she might, she couldn't judge him too harshly; she came with a whole set of baggage herself. What a pair they made, both running from violence into even more violence. Lydia looked back at Dean, he was running his fingers through his hair and pacing up and down. He hadn't looked this wound-up since disaster first struck the house. What house? Lydia's chest physically hurt when she remembered the charred ruins of their dream home. Dean had plunged every cent he had into the place, now they had nothing to show for it.

Suddenly, Dean stopped dead in his tracks and then turned toward Lydia. He pulled his phone from his pocket and flicked at the screen with his finger. He stared intently at the glow of the screen, whipping, apparently, through page after page of something or other. After a time, his expression became one of victory.

"That's him! I meant to delete all these photos, but I put it off then forgot about it."

"Forgot about what?"

"Look at this," Dean said, pointing the phone at Lydia.

Lydia laid eyes on a pic of some bikers, gathered together at some sort of function.

"This is a meet from years ago. Look at the dude with his arm around the porn-star looking woman... actually, I think she really *was* a porn-star," Dean enthused.

"Yeah. He looks like a cheery fellow," Lydia remarked, studying the man's pock-marked face and greasy, overgrown moustache.

"Missing a finger."

"Oh, yeah. I thought his hand looked odd. Wait... Dean, I've seen him before."

"Where?"

"At the hospital. He was watching me."

"His last name is Kelly."

"Okay."

"Kelly! He said, as though the name meant something.

"Who's that?" Lydia asked, perplexed.

Dean marched over to Lydia and pulled her to him, as though he could hear the traffic of her mind. He kissed her and caressed her cheek with a calloused hand.

"Everything's going to be okay. I'm not going to let anyone hurt you. Ever," Dean said emphatically.

The creaking of the screen door, followed by the thud of footsteps down onto the back lawn, gave Lydia goosebumps, but she wasn't sure why.

"Busy night at Bri's house!" announced Ben, his flip-flops slapping against the soles of his feet as he wandered across the grass with Danica following closely behind.

"Not really a good time, mate," Dean riposted, still looking at Lydia.

"You have party and not invite us?" Danica said in an accusatory tone.

"Sweetheart!" Ben scolded, shooting Danica a derisive look. "You alright Lydia? We just came over to check on you," he said.

"Yeah, no big deal. I get kidnapped and nearly burnt to death so often, it's become kind of dull," Lydia responded in a monotone.

"So long as you can laugh about it," Ben shot back.

"What can we do for you, mate? You made it clear you were sick of working on the house, before. Now you'll be happy to know, there's no house left to work on," Dean rumbled, his jaw clenching.

Ben stopped in front of Dean and Lydia, Danica standing to his right, her hand fanned over a protruding hip.

"Don't be like that, Dean-o. I was tired that day, mate... a little moody. Sorry about all that business. I actually wanted to talk to you about the house. I've got a tip on some budget-priced timber and some other stuff. Thought we could get things moving again."

Dean wrapped an arm around Lydia and turned to stare Ben in the face. "I don't know about that, mate," he replied.

"Come on, Dean-o. Let me make it up to you."

"The day we met, in the bike shop in town, you were chatting to the bloke delivering parts," Dean queried, placing a finger to his temple as though he were trying to prize the memory out of his skull.

"Yeah, that was Dingo," Ben offered. Danica shot a glance back at the house and looked back to find Lydia glowering at her.

"Well, you say that. I remembered recently that he used to go by the name of Dan. Dan Kelly: your half-brother," Dean said walking over to Ben so that the two men were standing dangerously close.

"Daniel? Nah, he's-" Ben muttered before Dean cut him off.

"Dan Kelly. Missing an index finger. Tattoo of the bullet that blew it off behind the knuckle. Threw the head of my..." Dean's voice broke and he closed his eyes and turned his head.

"Vhat you sayingk?" Danica quizzed feebly.

"What *are* you saying, Dean?" Lydia goaded, urging him to continue.

"I'm saying you better talk fast, dickhead!" Dean growled into Ben's face.

Ben ran his hand around the waist-band of his shorts, reaching for something unseen. Danica took a step back and Lydia advanced on her.

"We're gonna' head off, ladies and gents," announced Rangi, plodding down the steps, tiny Faye following him, gripping his hand.

"You got a new girlfriend there?" Kitty jibed, following behind.

Faye turned to smile goofily at Kitty.

Lydia shot Dean a concerned look and Ben glanced at Danica in a similar fashion. Ben pulled a handgun and pointed it at Dean and then Rangi and back again.

"Whoa! No need for that, Bro! You don't even know me!" Rangi shouted, pushing Faye behind him and stepping in front of her protectively.

"Shut up, 'Bro'!" Ben yelled back derisively.

Danica produced a smaller gun from her handbag and she and Ben stood back to back, covering both sides of the yard in practiced fashion.

"All you parasites, just calm down," Danica asserted, losing her Ukrainian accent and unexpectedly speaking in an Australian drawl.

"Listen to Debbie. She's not kidding," Ben said, pointing his weapon at Rangi.

"Debbie? What happened to Danica?" Lydia quizzed, trying to buy time.

"She's available anytime you want her, dah-link," Debbie oozed.

"Why would I-" began Lydia.

"I was talking to Dean," Debbie added.

"Nah, I'll pass," Dean responded.

"You can't tell me you haven't jerked it to this?" Debbie said, sticking out a hip and running a hand over it.

"Don't talk like that!" Ben yelled at Debbie over his shoulder.

"You tried to kill the woman I love. I'm gonna' hurt you," Dean sneered.

"Doesn't look that way, does it? Anyway, it all went a bit wrong, mate. You were meant to be taken down as well, but you went on a little ride, didn't you? Had to scramble to get the Vamps to do a bit of damage control. You made me look like a right twit."

"You *are* a right twit. Would never have taken you for a gang twit though."

"I would have pegged you as a deserter. Even if I hadn't been told. Who calls their MC a 'gang'?"

"That's all it was in the end."

"It's disrespectful!" Ben screamed.

"Why not just shoot me?" Dean queried.

"Nah, you were always meant to be delivered to the Boys. Dan knew you as soon as he saw you, based on your description. Chapters all up and down the coast were told to look out for you. Brando from the Boys had a feeling you might end up this way, though. He knew more about you than he ever let on. He's a wise old fart, that Brando. I'm sure he'll have a laundry list of fun stuff ready for you when you see him. I heard he melted a bloke's balls to the exhaust of his own hog once, after he found out the prick was a squealer. Lyds over here is a different story, but I don't take orders from no-"

Brianna surreptitiously pushed open the screen door and let out a scream as soon as she saw the gun pointed in Faye's direction.

"Don't do anything stupid!" Ben screamed at her.

Brianna began to hyperventilate, sinking down and rocking on her haunches, tears streaming down her face.

"Now here's what we're gonna' do. We're all getting in that big truck of Deans and we're gonna' go for a drive," Debbie said, a little arousal seeping into her voice.

"I'm steering this ship!" Ben asserted.

"You waste too much time," Debbie shot back, her weapon still trained on Dean and Lydia. "That's why I'm rooting Dan. You're a pussy."

"What? You little slut! Does Uncle Steve know?" Ben replied angrily.

"Uncle Steve? Wait. Are you two... related?" Lydia asked.

"None of your business, moll!" Debbie barked.

"Oh my God. You are!" Lydia responded, smiling with satisfaction.

"Look, you shut it, or I'll make you shut it!" Ben exclaimed, losing focus for an instant.

Rangi took the opportunity to lunge at Ben, pushing his gun-hand aside and landing an uppercut to the man's jaw. As Debbie looked back to see what the fuss was, Lydia pounced on her, thrusting a knee into her stomach, forcing her to drop her weapon. Lydia elbowed Debbie's face as Ben shook off Rangi's blow, long enough to smash his pistol against the young man's temple. Rangi went down, hard. As Lydia tussled with Debbie, Dean made a run at her weapon, but Ben spun around and pulled the slide back on his gun, the sound stopping Dean in his tracks. Lydia put her hands up to indicate surrender and Debbie hobbled over to pick up her pistol.

Faye began to sob and Brianna stumbled down the steps to her side. Brianna reached out to embrace her daughter, when Debbie loomed up and pushed Brianna back onto the steps. She grabbed Faye by the hair, making the little girl scream.

"Alright, the stupidity ends now!" Debbie yelled as she pointed the gun at Faye's face.

Debbie eyed Kitty off, indicating with a sweep of her head, that she should join Dean and Lydia. Kitty looked down at Rangi, lying on the grass unconscious. Her face crumpled as she made her way over to her sister.

"Maybe we just execute these bastards here," Ben said to Debbie, before spitting blood out onto the grass.

Brianna let out a wail and Debbie smiled darkly, pulling harder on Faye's hair for added cruelty.

Debbie bent down and picked Faye up by the ankle, yanking her up and down. "Look how light you are! I could throw you like a frisbee, couldn't I? Or I could slap you against a tree, like a bird with a stupid little worm. Can you count to ten, honey?" she asked Faye, glaring at Lydia.

"Don't do this!" Dean boiled.

"Well, answer the lady!" Ben chimed in.

"Mum!" Faye cried.

"I'm here, baby," Brianna whimpered.

"Tell the brat to do what I say!" Debbie squawked.

Brianna looked to Dean, silently imploring him to do something.

"Tell her!" Debbie yelled impatiently. A gust of wind surged through the trees in the yard, mirroring Debbie's temperament.

Lydia looked longingly over the fence to the neighbor's house, but there was no activity. People in the street were either driving off to stay with friends and family in safer locations, or they had secured shutters and reinforcements and were holed up indoors. The growing tempest was muffling the sounds of the altercation in Brianna's yard and there was no one around to bear witness and call the cops. Ben and Debbie could quite possibly get away with murder, barring further resistance. Lydia looked at Faye, her expression one of abject terror, the kind only a child can feel, and it drove a spike into her heart.

"Faye!" Lydia called out. Debbie looked over, appeased that someone was going to coach the child on playing her little game.

Lydia looked over at Rangi. "Show Debbie the starfish," she requested.

Faye extended her arms and placed her hands on the ground, she wrenched her leg from Debbie's grasp and cartwheeled away from the woman. Debbie pointed her gun at Faye for a moment, before Rangi swept her legs out from under her. Ben spun around and Dean converged on him, grabbed his right arm and struck the elbow, a sickening 'pop' making Ben squeal like a frightened pig. Debbie had landed on her back, knocking the wind out of her and Rangi took the opportunity to scoop up her gun. Dean pointed Ben's gun at his forehead. Brianna ran over to Faye and picked her up, squeezing her tight. Kitty bolted over to Rangi and threw herself against him. Lydia, her face dark and full of rage, stormed over to Debbie and picked her up by the scruff of her thin, tight-fitting, lycra top. She landed punch after punch on the woman's face. Lydia pulled her dyed hair and shook her violently.

"Do you like that? Do you? Answer me!" Lydia howled, before kneeing Debbie in the stomach.

"Lydia!" Dean yelled, making her freeze.

Lydia released Debbie and looked back at Dean, her eyes glazed over as though she was in a trance. Everyone stared at her and the wind moaned like a chorus of lost souls. Dean gripped the back of Ben's neck and he pulled the man's face close to his own.

"You and Debbie or Danica or whatever the hell her name is, leave here now! You tell the Vampyres that we're not intimidated," Dean spat, before throwing Ben back to the ground.

Ben crawled back to his feet and dusted himself off. "You know, it was hard work pretending to like you, day after day. I had to choke back the desire to cave your head in with a hammer, or shoot you with a nail-gun, every minute. You're a dog for leaving the Boys. If I ditched the Vamps like you ditched your crew? I'd expect to be torn limb from limb," Ben proclaimed, spitting afterward.

"You may get your wish, when they see that you couldn't close the deal," Dean shot back.

"It's all a bit more complicated than that, mate," Ben oozed, glaring at Lydia.

"Get outta' here. Before I shoot you in the face, you gutless bastard," Dean declared.

"It's all gonna' catch up with you. Come on Debs," Ben ordered.

Dean and Rangi followed Ben and Debbie up the side of the house and watched them ride away on Ben's bike, before retiring to Brianna's dining room. Dean took the gun off Rangi and stowed it with Ben's gun, atop a tall shelf unit.

"You'll need to leave now," Dean stated, looking back and forth between Rangi, Brianna and Kitty.

Faye hugged Dean's legs and then Lydia's. Kitty hugged her sister vigorously and Brianna kissed her brother's cheek.

"Take care of yourself, D," she whispered, before squeezing Lydia tightly. "And you. Thank you," she said, before kissing Lydia goodbye.

"I'll see you soon," Kitty said with a quivery voice.

"Of course you will," Lydia responded.

The party of four piled into Rangi's sleek, black hatchback and Faye pressed her face to the rear window as they sped away. Dean immediately closed and locked the front door and he and Lydia proceeded to lock all the windows. Dean then grabbed the weapons and popped each magazine in turn, checking the available rounds.

"Each gun has a full clip," he said seriously.

Lydia saluted him earnestly and then kissed him. "What now?" she queried.

"Now we batten down them hatches, bro," Dean quipped. They both laughed, despite the looming darkness.

Chapter Six:

The Fortress

The evening was spent checking the kitchen and bathroom for useable items and chemicals. Lydia and Dean purposefully dug holes, prepared things that would burn and stab and immobilize. They kept kitchen knives and tools within reach, but hidden from view. They secured and fortified weak entry points with fallen fence palings, rationed their food and supplies and slept in shifts. Dean completed set after set of chin-ups from a bar secured in the doorway of the guest bedroom and Lydia practiced Muay Thai in the wee hours of the morning, when she wasn't on watch. They checked the news for any word on trouble nearby and for updates on the coming tropical storm-front. Dean even set up Faye's old baby-monitor to listen for intruders in the backyard. Lydia would paw over old, paper street-maps, laid out on the dining table. She and Dean would mark out potential escape routes and speculate on where their assailants might be coming from. Sometimes, Lydia would just walk from room to room, checking and re-checking the improvised barricades until she knew every plank and nail intimately. Two days went by, then a third and on the fourth day, Lydia awoke from her allotted sleep period, to a disturbing text message from an old friend.

"What is it?" Dean asked, sensing Lydia's concern.

"Officer Barnes. He's been trying to call. Mason's charges... they were thrown out. It was a technicality. The arrest... Barnes is under investigation now. Mason's free," Lydia said bleakly, her blood running cold.

"He doesn't know where you are," Dean stated calmly.

"No. There's no way. Still should have killed him when I had the chance," Lydia pronounced grimly.

"You did the right thing letting him live. Killing is never an option."

"It was for him!"

"And do you want to be like him?"

"Of course I don't. What do you mean?"

"Remember how you reacted, when I beat up on those guys in front of you after we'd first met?"

"Yes. I probably overreacted. I accused you of treating violence like a drug. I have to admit, I think I get it now," Lydia said, staring past Dean's face.

"You wanted to annihilate Debbie. You were possibly going to."

"So? Should I be a helpless lamb forever? Should I let people stomp on me? Hurt the people I care for?"

"No. Never."

"Then what are you saying?"

"You made me rethink who I wanted to be. I'm better because of you. Don't let people like... him, drag you down. You're better than that, Lydia."

"Maybe I don't want to be better anymore. Maybe taking the high road is what gets innocent people killed. Like Dora. Like your niece."

"She's okay now."

"Yeah. Right now."

"Why would you say that?" Dean demanded.

"Forget it."

Lydia walked away, unlocked the back door and stormed down the stairs to the yard. Dean exhaled forcefully, made for the kitchen and pulled open the fridge door. He whipped out a beer, popped the top and drained it in one chug. After throwing the can across the room into the sink, he cocked his head to one side. The rumble of motorcycles sent his senses into overdrive. Dean grabbed the handguns and ran to the backdoor to find Lydia already back inside, securing the locks. He threw her a weapon and the two of them systematically re-checked every potential entry point. The house was high enough to deter access via most of the windows, but there were a few with adverse potential.

The wind howled and the house creaked. Lydia and Dean posted themselves at the front of the house, not yet hazarding a look outside. Dean could hear the bikes pulling up and engines being switched off. It sounded like only three, probably the three that had pursued him, including one: Dan Kelly. Not long after, there came the sound of a car pulling up outside, something large, like a station wagon. A door opened and then was slammed shut before a man called out.

"Lydiaaaaaaaaaaaaaaaaaaa!" bellowed Mason.

Lydia's eyes widened and she looked at the floor for a moment. After a while, she peered through a slit in the wooden shutters to see the very person she dreaded most in the world. He wore an uncharacteristically ratty black tee shirt and blue jeans. His black hair had been buzz cut and his thick beard had been cut down to a long goatee. His short stay in custody had clearly had an impact on him. The man looked stronger than ever, but there was something else: a strange look in his blue eyes. Mason had always been fearsome, but now he had a kind of Charles Manson energy about him. Lydia looked away. She gripped her pistol tight and closed her eyes.

"Hey. It's going to be alright," Dean said, snapping Lydia back to reality.

"How the hell did he find me?"

"He's out there with members of the local MC. I don't think that's a coincidence."

"Christ. The last thing we need is *him* teaming up with *them*!"

"Look. I've got a bad feeling about this. It might be time to throw caution to the wind and call the cops," stated Dean.

"We do that and it's you and me who go to jail," Lydia shot back.

Dean looked down at the gun in his hands. "I don't want you to get hurt, lady."

"I don't want to see you hurt either," Lydia added.

"Come out Lydia! I just want to talk!" Mason barked.

Lydia peered outside again. The bikers had dismounted and two of them pulled shotguns from their bikes; the third one held the largest handgun that Lydia had ever seen. Lydia stood up dutifully and pulled her phone from the pocket of her jeans, she dialed and waited. After what felt like forever, a female voice answered, "Detective Crowe."

Mason pounded on the back door again, but there was no answer. He and his three allies had walked down the side of the house to the rear in case anyone was watching. The neighborhood was a ghost town, but Mason wanted to ensure there would be no interruptions. The Gods had granted him freedom and opportunities so that he could fulfill his destiny as the Great Beast. He was a beast that demanded blood sacrifice and what better offering than the lamb cowering behind closed doors, awaiting her judgement. He could taste Lydia's fear, her quivering body begged for his touch. His touch would elevate her; she would be more than just a partner, a girlfriend or a companion. She was destined to be a holy sacrament; a morsel destined to allow him to realize his God status. He would take his place amongst the very deities that had led him to her. The Beast God.

"You can't lock me out of your life, Lydia! When we last met, I was just like you. I was weak and feeble and I did not know the way! Things have aligned now, my love. I bring gifts and blessings! The lamb that hides from the great bear only knows fear! Once its destiny has been fulfilled, then things become as they should and the universe rejoices! Offer yourself to me willingly and your new man may walk away unharmed!"

"Bullshit to that!" exclaimed Dan.

"Shut your mouth!" scolded Mason.

"If you do not open the door willingly, you will rouse the anger of the Beast! It will be worse than any outpouring of rage you have ever experienced! I will take you and penetrate you and tear the flesh from your bones. I will drink your blood and devour your meaty parts and you will know true terror!"

"You want me to shoot the prick open?" queried Dan, scratching his belly with the muzzle of his Five-Hundred Magnum.

Mason yelled back at the man without looking at him. "I don't need your help! Wait until I call on you."

Dan mumbled something obscene under his breath before Mason closed his eyes, raised his upturned palms heavenward and kicked at the door. He kicked it again and again before all hell broke loose in the yard.

"Detective Crowe! Drop your weapons and put your hands out where I can see them!" yelled the sturdy woman, her gun drawn and trained on Mason and Dan respectively.

Detective Lee covered the other two bikers, bent legged and cautiously approaching his targets.

"Do what we ask! Drop the bloody weapons!" howled Detective Lee.

"Don't take orders from gooks," said one of the bikers.

"Yeah, well, you'll take orders from this one," replied Lee.

"You little dim-sim sucking maggot. You know we'll get out anyway. The justice system's a fun-park ride."

A shot rang out, then another. Detective Lee fell to the ground as one biker discharged his shotgun whilst pretending to lower it to the ground. Lee's face was covered in blood, his Kevlar vest of little use. Detective Crowe fired on the shooter, winging him and causing him to release his grip on the weapon. Dan fired an enormous round from his Magnum into Detective Crowe's exposed shoulder and she fell to her knees, groaning in agony. Mason launched himself from the top of the steps onto Detective Crowe like a panther. He punched her in the jaw, then grabbing the side of her head, he slammed her face into the ground, again and again. Once the woman stopped moving, Mason, satisfied that the job was done, hunched over the Detective, sniffing her. Dan laughed maniacally and one of the bikers walked over to check on Detective Lee, shaking his head at Dan to indicate that the man was dead.

Mason stepped away from Crowe's body, his hands spattered with her blood. He stared at the crimson streams that began to run down his fingers, over his wrists and forearms and he grinned. Licking his fingers, he released a moan of pleasure, before staring at the biker that Detective Crowe had shot.

"Is that one... functional?" Mason enquired coldly.

"My name's Baz. I'm fine prick-face," the bleeding biker spat.

"Okay, Baz. Time to hunt. The woman's mine. Do what you want to the man."

Baz and Dan looked at each other. The third biker stomped toward the side of the house, staring at the ground.

"Where are you going, Mooney?" called Dan.

"This is some bull-crap. I'm out," replied Mooney.

"You leave now, Moon-o, you pay the price."

"I don't care," called Mooney already disappearing.

Suddenly, the back door flew open and Lydia appeared, brandishing a bottle with cloth in its neck, a bottle that she now ignited with a lighter. She threw the object and it landed near Baz, sending the leather-clad man reeling backwards. Baz's booted feet haphazardly dropped into a ditch, disguised with grass clippings. The man screamed as rusty nails, hammered through a fence post, pierced the soles of his footwear, and his flesh. Dan fired his gun at Lydia in response, but she deftly dove out of the way. Mason smacked Dan's weapon down.

"What did I say?" Mason rumbled.

"Look what the bitch did to Baz!" he replied. Baz lay on the ground and he winced and screamed as he pulled nails from his feet.

Mason grabbed Dan by the lapels of his leather vest and drew him close.

"I'm the Beast God. You are an acolyte. Don't get mixed up."

"You're a psycho, is what you are," Dan retorted.

Dean appeared at the door suddenly, with his weapon extended. He fired in Dan and Mason's direction, causing them to duck for cover. Dan chuckled evilly.

"You're a lousy shot, mate!" he called out, looking up at the point of impact in the looming camphor-laurel tree. Suddenly, liquid began trickling into Dan's eyes as Mason backed away. Dan screamed as the substance burnt his eyes severely. The man scratched at his face desperately, falling face-first into the grass and writhing like a fish on the rocks.

"It's time for my ascension!" Mason proclaimed into the air, as he picked up Dan's gun and rushed for the back door.

He crouched at the top step and took a furtive glance inside, before ducking into the first bedroom to the right. Propping himself against the bed, Mason scrutinized his surroundings and soon realized, he was in Lydia's bedroom. This was the room she probably shared with that weakling, surrendering her lotus flower to him, a pale simulacrum of the man she was meant to be with. Mason recognized Lydia's underwear peeking out of one of the dresser drawers and he lurched over to retrieve a pair. Plain and black and modestly cut; at least some things hadn't changed. He buried his nose in the silky material and inhaled, anticipating the ritual he had imagined in his cell, countless times. He would allow her the privilege of being anointed by the only celestial being she would ever meet in person. Then, when he had absorbed her life into his being, he would burn her body and his own. He had jerry cans full of gasoline in the back of the station-wagon. Her lover, well maybe Mason would break his arms and legs and lay his ruined body out, so he could watch; the funeral pyre would be only for Mason and Lydia.

Mason crept to the bedroom door and looked out. He heard creaking and shuffling up near the front of the house. The Beast's hearing was like that of a wolf, his eyesight was like an eagle's and his strength rivalled the largest of bears'. He stood up to full height, fearing nothing. He would not need the mortal weapon he had picked up in a moment of remembered human frailty. He dropped the large hand gun on the floor and strutted up the hallway, like the proud animal he was. His one-man procession must have been glorious, Mason assumed it was, even though he lacked the outsider perspective. He raised his head aloft, and that's when his foot sunk into the floor. The floorboards gave way and his right leg dropped out from under him making Mason fall sideways. His groin was wrenched and a shooting pain stabbed his abdomen. These underlings were trying to trap the Beast!

Mason struggled to free himself from the improvised trapdoor and Dean took the opportunity to move in on him. He pulled the big man to his feet, before landing one, two, three punches to Mason's stomach. Mason hobbled awkwardly, but managed to wrap his large hands around Dean's throat, lifting him off the ground. He choked the man, hard, then threw him against the wall. Lydia smacked Mason in the head with the handle of her gun. Mason, barely registering the impact, smashed her right hand into the wall and Lydia lost the weapon. He thrust the flat of his hand into her chest, sending her skidding along the wooden floor like a discarded ragdoll. Dean came at him again, spear-tackling Mason, the two of them hitting the floor like a ton of bricks.

"No gun, little man?" Mason grunted.

"You're not going out that easily," Dean growled, jabbing Mason in the face repeatedly.

Mason rolled Dean over, pinning him to the ground and he drew his arm back. Lydia wrapped a knotted rope around Mason's thick neck and pulled tight. The man's face was soon the color of pinot noir, his forehead a maze of protruding veins. Lydia inhaled deeply, relaxed her shoulders for a second and pulled the rope tighter, giving it everything she had. Dean propped himself up against the wall and stumbled before standing upright. He kicked Mason in the side, again and again before the man appeared to be nearing unconsciousness. Mason's eyes bulged and saliva streamed out of the corners of his mouth. Lydia's strength was flagging and Dean moved forward to assist her. Just then, Mason summoned his remaining power, snapping his body forward, sending Lydia flying over his head into Dean. Mason coughed and spluttered, rubbing his throat with one hand, and reaching for the wall with the other.

Before she knew what was happening, Mason had picked up Lydia and disappeared into the kitchen with her. Dean, ignoring his body's protests, gave chase to find the large man hunched over Lydia, one of their hidden blades in his hand.

Mason pressed the knife against Lydia's belly. "The Beast knows all your hiding places. He sees all. Your schemes are funny and pathetic. Don't come too close, mortal," he growled.

"You want to do this again?" Dean queried, his eyes locking onto Lydia's.

"There is no 'again'. You're too trapped in your fleshly form to actually see what this is."

"Explain it to me," Dean replied, buying time.

"Your feeble mind could never absorb it all. I would fill you with my intentions and your fragile psyche would pop like a balloon."

"Well, maybe you can't explain it because you're full of crap."

"I am the end of all things!"

"You're not though, are you?"

"You don't know what it is to aspire to God status. You'll never see past your own experiences. You touch everything with a gloved hand. You never really have contact with the greater reality."

"Like you used to make contact with Lydia. Hitting her like a weakling?"

"That was my old life."

"Looks a lot like the new one mirrors the old."

"No. I'm going to eject my sacred seed into this offering. I'm going to devour her eyes and see the vast emptiness of the mortal human condition. Then I'm going to cut her open, bury my face in her innards and look out across eternity before I give the both of us over to the purifying power of the holy pyre."

"Sounds like you've snapped. You're just a quivering mess, hiding behind this ridiculous story you've told yourself," retorted Dean.

"You should bow down and show some reverence!" spat Mason, pushing the knife against Lydia's abdomen.

Dean, swallowed his fear. Seeing Mason's outburst, he pushed harder. "You're terrified that you're not just a regular guy, you're less than that."

"I'm more than you'll ever know!"

"But no one ever will know, will they? It's easy to say you're meant for better things and then, what? You burn yourself so that no evidence is necessary? That's a cop out, man." Dean goaded.

"You don't-"

"Understand? Yeah, you said that."

Mason stood up to full height and turned away from Lydia. His eyes bulged and sweat trickled down his temples.

Snapping his arm back, suddenly, he threw the knife at Dean, the blade wedging into his thigh. Dean pulled the weapon out of his flesh and turned to lead Mason away from Lydia. He had made it halfway down the hall when he felt one of Mason's fleshy hands make a grab for his shirt. Dean was yanked backward, spinning around to try and fight the large man off. Mason grabbed at Dean's throat and Dean took the opportunity to stab him with the knife still dripping with his own blood. Mason wrapped his sausage fingers around Dean's wrist and twisted hard. The knife fell to the ground.

Lydia threw her body at Mason from behind. He spun around, without releasing his grip on Dean, deflecting her down the corridor toward the backdoor.

"You will accept your part in this," Mason oozed.

"You need to die!" Lydia sneered.

"Your blood is payment for everything after. As a living creature, you're worthless. As my sacrifice, you will be part of a greater whole that activates the universe!"

Dean took the opportunity to wrench himself free, throwing his weight at Mason, the larger man barely budging. Mason looked furious, swollen and barely human. Dean's feet were soon off the ground. He was bounced back and forth between the walls of the hallway as plaster cracked and fell to the floor. Lydia screamed as Mason threw Dean around like a grizzly, breaking the body of its prey. Lydia couldn't believe that she was in the same situation again and she was going to watch the man she loved die at the hands of the man she hated with every cell; then she saw the huge Magnum lying on the floor. It had fallen in the doorway of her bedroom and it looked formidable. Lydia scrambled over and scooped up the weapon. In that moment, she was grateful for the time Dean had spent with her at the shooting range, back south. Lydia aimed the piece at Mason, pulled back the hammer and felt the unexpected sensation of hands grabbing her from behind.

Baz pawed at Lydia, ripping the gun out of her hands and bringing it down against the side of her head. Lydia slumped against the wall as the biker pushed the muzzle of the weapon against her chest, chuckling suggestively as he traced the curve of her cleavage with the cold steel. Lydia tugged at the neckline of her top, revealing more skin. Baz smiled lewdly, the stupid man clearly anticipating some sort of erotic adventure amidst the chaos. Lydia whipped a foot upward, knocking the gun from Baz's hands. Her body spun like a top and another kick found the biker's head, pushing him backward, over the balustrade of the rear stairs. The man landed with a dull 'thud' and he didn't move afterward.

Lydia turned to see Mason's continuing assault on Dean.

"Stop! Please!" She pleaded.

"Give yourself to me!" Mason cried.

Looking at Dean's blood covered face, Lydia nodded. "Okay."

Mason let out a yell as blood poured from his cheek, running down his neck and soaking his shirt. A knife jutted out of the side of Mason's face, a knife carved of bone. Mason reached for the blade, but Dean kicked him in the belly, sending him hurtling backward, into the dining room. Dean advanced, pummeling the man with blow after blow. He slammed Mason up against a window and rained punches on his already bloody face. The big man pulled the knife from his cheek and tried to slash at Dean with it, but Dean adroitly snatched the blade from his opponent, jamming it between Mason's ribs. Mason tried to gather himself up, but before he could, Dean was airborne, launching both feet into Mason's chest. Mason was propelled through the make-shift barriers securing the windows, through the glass, and onto the verandah.

Lydia ran at Dean, wrapping herself around him, peppering his face with kisses.

"Okay, lady. It's not over yet," Dean said woozily.

"There's no way he's coming back from that whooping!" Lydia enthused.

"You better check on those cops out back. I'll check on Goliath out there," Dean instructed.

"Be careful. Please," Lydia said emphatically.

Dean nodded, before searching for his gun and Lydia ran out to the backyard. She pounded down the steps and her eyes fell on the ruined face of Detective Lee. It was clear that the man had died protecting her and she felt deeply guilty. The other Detective was lying face down, there was blood, but Lydia desperately hoped for the best. She rolled the woman over, ripped off her Kevlar vest, and leant in to check on Crowe's breathing; there was nothing. Lydia began the CPR she had learnt back in the States, when her mom had first taken a turn for the worse. After many chest compressions, when Lydia had begun to lose hope, Detective Crowe began coughing and spluttering. Lydia sighed with relief and sat with the Detective, reassuring her. Lydia pulled her cell from her pocket, but it was well and truly ruined. She felt around in the Detective's jacket for a working phone, and called for an ambulance.

Dean had only just begun undoing the locks on the front door, when he heard the sound of an engine turning over. He couldn't believe his ears, surely it was a neighbor, Mason had to be out for the count. Dean burst out onto the verandah and to his chagrin, Mason was jerkily backing away in his wagon. Dean ran down the stairs, dashed for his truck and sped after the man. There was no way he was going to let Mason escape. The station-wagon powered north, swerving across the road clumsily. Dean was feeling fatigued and groggy himself, but his will was bent on his target. Dean accelerated, ramming Mason's vehicle, making the wagon fishtail. A fierce wind sent a huge, gnarled tree branch, crashing onto the road between the two vehicles. Dean swerved hard, his tires squealing. Mason gained some headway and Dean pushed his pickup as far as he could, but the heavy, old truck had trouble chewing up the gap.

Dean began to visualize the pain that Mason had caused Lydia. He saw Mason striking the woman he loved, beating her mercilessly. Dean gripped the steering wheel tight and he felt as though he might push the accelerator through the floor of the truck with white-hot rage. The distance between his car and Mason's began to diminish; Dean hoped it was due to blood-loss. He pictured Lydia, smiling back at him, her beautiful eyes glinting in the tropical sun. He had wanted to take her pain away, protect her from any and all threats and dedicate his life to making her happy. Dean realized then and there, that none of that could happen whilst Mason walked the earth. Lydia had been right all along: he needed disposing of, like waste-wood.

Dean gained on Mason just enough, so that he could pull up alongside the wagon, on its right side. He fired a shot at Mason, smashing glass and making the man duck for cover. A second shot grazed Mason's shoulder, causing him to drift toward Dean's pickup. Dean slowed slightly and pulled the wheel violently, hitting the rear of Mason's vehicle with the edge of his bull-bar. Mason's car began to oversteer and the cyclonic wind hurled a spear-like sapling at Mason's windshield. The young tree pierced the glass and grazed Mason's face, making him cry out. Mason was sent into a spin and Dean hurtled forward, t-boning him into a tree on the side of the road. The station-wagon crumpled up against the trunk of the thick eucalypt. Dean's truck lurched forward with sheer force of impact, the rear tires leaving the ground for a moment, before slamming back down again. Mason struggled to get free as Dean fought to open his driver-side door, finally kicking it ajar. He jumped out of his vehicle and his left leg buckled. He limped over to Mason's door, pulling at it as the man also threw his might into getting free. Metal groaned as the door burst open, Mason lunging at Dean, picking him up and slamming him into the wreckage. The blade was still jutting out of his rib-cage, but he seemed unaware of it. Dean swept Mason's feet out from under him and positioned himself atop the man's chest. He punched and punched Mason's face, like a man possessed. Mason grabbed Dean's thighs and swung him against the wagon. Dean's eyes glazed over; something didn't feel right. A spike of twisted metal pierced Dean's shoulder. Dean rocked back and forth to get free, crying out in agony and Mason finally saw the bone-knife in his flesh. He pulled it out and stared at the bloody blade.

"I'm the sacrifice," Mason slurred. The large man's knees gave way and he fell, face-first into the dirt.

The fire started almost immediately, spreading from Dean's engine to Mason's gas can laden station-wagon. The flames burned furiously and relentlessly, consuming everything in their path.

Epilogue

Lydia felt like she had left her body as she floated up the stairs to meet with Detective Crowe. Someone greeted her and directed her to the correct office, but Lydia felt like she only *looked* like a flesh and blood human, responding and understanding things. She took the seat that Crowe offered her and she accepted the offer of coffee as it seemed like the thing to do. In reality, Lydia floated above herself, looking down and wondering what her avatar felt, if anything at all.

When the incident occurred at Brianna's house,

some nights ago now, her soul had clearly been pushed out of her corporeal form. Maybe it was to protect her from being engulfed by unbearable amounts of shock and grief and pain, so much pain. She was grateful that she was disconnected. It was like being put under anesthesia before surgery. Part of her feared waking, seeing the horror of her chest cavity, her heart exposed to the world.

"I want to thank you for what you did for me," the Detective said, her gaze fixed on Lydia.

"Don't mention it. It's too much to take in, isn't it?" Lydia said slowly, like she was reciting someone else's words.

"Well, you saved my life. I hope you understand that. I guess you'll want me to get to the point, though."

"Okay," Lydia said mechanically.

"The crash-site. Our guys scoured the area. Examined both vehicles as best they could."

"What did they find?" Lydia asked, in a voice that sounded like it came from someone else.

"This is... I know it's not what you want to hear. There were remains amongst the wreckage. The fire was so severe, it's been hard to pin down and confirm the identities of the two parties involved. We don't doubt that both... individuals, would have been consumed. A fire fueled by that amount of petrol, would have burned hotter than a furnace. Dental records are proving impossible to nail down but... well, somehow, they found this," Detective Crowe said, proffering a plastic evidence bag to Lydia. The bone-knife was blackened by soot, but Lydia recognized it immediately. She had changed in the time she and Dean had been together. She wasn't the weepy mess she was when their worlds had first collided. Seeing the very thing she had given Dean, the object that in the back of her mind was meant to be a protective talisman, made something snap inside of her. Lydia felt like her soul had been violently smashed back into her body. Everything she had blocked out, all the pain, came at once and she wasn't sure she could survive it.

Lydia fell forward, off of her seat onto her knees. She cried and wailed so hard, she thought she might pass out. Detective Crowe got up and walked around her desk to Lydia. The larger woman picked Lydia up effortlessly and cradled her in her thick arms. Lydia wept and buried her face in Crowe's bosom. The Detective stroked Lydia's hair and rocked side to side with her and that familiar white noise hissed in Lydia's ears.

Kitty pulled the ceramic urn from the camping backpack she'd brought it in. The sun was dipping and the water of Flying Fish Point was stained blood-red. Parrots cried out in flocks, their shrieking carrying across the water eerily.

"You made it, Mom," Lydia said through teary eyes, gripping the urn alongside her sister.

"We love you. We miss you and we'll always remember you," Kitty added, her voice breaking mid-sentence.

Lydia lifted the lid of the receptacle and the pair gently tipped it, releasing a cloud of ash over and into the water. Lydia handed off the urn to Kitty, who put it back into the pack, slinging it over her shoulder. Water lapped at their ankles and the weather was much calmer after Cyclone Dora, unexpectedly, decided to give Innisfail a wide berth. Lydia looked at Kitty and then out to sea. Kitty hugged her tight.

"I know, Lydia. I know," Kitty said, rubbing her sister's back.

"Don't you leave me!" Lydia cried into Kitty's shoulder.

"I'm here," Kitty answered.

"I don't know what to do," Lydia blurted, exasperated.

"We'll work it out together."

"I'm so happy you're with me."

"Hey, Listeria," Kitty said, pulling away from Lydia.

"What?"

"Did you know that there are three times as many people as there are sheep, living in Australia?"

"Really?" Lydia queried, wiping her eyes with the sleeves of her pullover.

"Yep."

"Did you get that from Mom?"

"Sure did."

"Then she's still here. Is that too corny?" Lydia queried.

"I think you're allowed a little corn right this instant."

"My friend, Dora, would have said something wise right about now. Probably something about the nature of the universe. She believed that some moments go on forever, echoing through time... I don't know, I can't articulate things like she used to. Maybe the same goes for people."

"Well, if Mom's here then, so is Dean," Kitty said, smiling warmly.

"That's truer than you realize," muttered Lydia.

"What does that mean?"

"Never mind. I'll tell you later. We should just absorb the ambience or something," Lydia countered.

"Nope. You're not getting off the hook. You know I'm going to interrogate you until you tell me anyway, so you may as well-"

Lydia interrupted. "I'm having his baby," she added wistfully, caressing her belly.

Kitty dropped the urn.

Don't miss out!

Visit the website below and you can sign up to receive emails whenever Kira Parke publishes a new book. There's no charge and no obligation.

https://books2read.com/r/B-A-KFEH-ZTMW

BOOKS 2 READ

Connecting independent readers to independent writers.